THE NEW
SUFFERINGS
OF
YOUNG W.

ULRICH PLENZDORF

THE NEW SUFFERINGS OF YOUNG W.

a novel

Translated by Kenneth P. Wilcox

FREDERICK UNGAR PUBLISHING CO.
NEW YORK

Translated from the German
Die neuen Leiden des jungen W.
by arrangement with the original publishers
© 1973 VEB Hinstorff Verlag, Rostock, GDR

Copyright © 1979 by Frederick Ungar Publishing Co., Inc.
Printed in the United States of America
Designed by Helen Roberts

Library of Congress Cataloging in Publication Data

Plenzdorf, Ulrich, 1934–
  The new sufferings of young W.

  Translation of Die neuen Leiden des jungen W.
  I. Title.
PZ4.P7255Ne [PT2676.L39]   833'.9'14   78-20928
ISBN 0-8044-2735-6
ISBN 0-8044-6656-4

Introduction

The young W. of this novel—whose name is Edgar Wibeau—finds some of his lost roots in Goethe's celebrated romantic hero. There is also another, unexpected influence on the young man. As Edgar puts it: "Whoever wrote [*Werther*] should read Salinger some time." For this young W. is even more a soul mate of Holden Caulfield; the Salinger influence entwined with that of Goethe is part of the fascination of reading Plenzdorf.

Ulrich Plenzdorf was born in Berlin in 1934. His parents were Communists, and like other members of the political left faced persecution in Hitler's Germany. Plenzdorf worked for three years, from 1955 to 1958, as a stagehand for DEFA (Deutsche Film-AG, the state-owned German Film Corporation), served in the military for a year, and then enrolled in a four-year course at the film academy in Babelsberg, completing his studies in 1963. Since then he has worked for DEFA as a scenarist and producer, and has written a number of screenplays.

Early in 1972 *Sinn und Form*, the leading literary magazine of the German Democratic Republic, printed a first draft of a novel by Plenzdorf, *Die neuen Leiden des jungen W.* (*The New Sufferings of Young W.*) the writer's first published work. In the following months there was a radio drama version and then a stage adaptation, which premièred at the state theater in Halle on May 18, 1972. In March of 1973 both VEB Hinstorff Verlag in Rostock (in the GDR) and Suhrkamp Verlag (in the Federal Republic of Germany) published a final draft of *The New Sufferings of Young W.*, again in novel form.

The work has been a tremendous success, making Plenzdorf the most popular author writing in the GDR since Brecht. Throngs of enthusiasts flocked to the theaters to see the play and to the bookstores to buy the novel. The years 1972 and 1973 were marked by an almost constant discussion, not just in GDR literary circles, but in the GDR populace at large, of Plenzdorf's work. Only a few weeks after the première in Halle, in June of 1972, *Forum*, the official organ of the Central Committee of the Free German Youth, the GDR's largest youth organization, published the transcript of a discussion of the play it had held with Wolfhilde Dierl, a lawyer, and Wolfgang Bachmann, a theater director.

So great, in fact, was the initial response to *The New Sufferings of Young W.* that *Sinn und Form* felt impelled to invite its readership to take part in a public discussion: On October 31, 1972, an open forum was held in the Academy of the Arts of the German Democratic Republic under the sponsorship of *Sinn und Form*, to which Plenzdorf himself was invited. The first question (of seven) on the agenda was: "What are the reasons for the unusual success of this work?" *Sinn und Form* was quickly followed by the two other GDR literary magazines of international repute. In 1973 *Neue Deutsche Literatur* printed an interview that two of its editorial staff had held with four youths—a schoolgirl, two university students, and an apprentice construction worker—about the success of the play, and a few months later *Akzente* printed a long series to the editor about the work in general.

Why was it (and is it still) so popular? To begin with, it is an extremely entertaining story told with considerable artistic skill. Edgar Wibeau, a really charming seventeen-year-old, the son of the director of the factory in which he is doing an apprenticeship, is a model all-GDR boy. One day he gets fed up with it all and suddenly drops out. He runs away to Berlin, where he hides out in an abandoned garden house owned by the parents of his best friend Willi, paints, dances, falls in love, and—in general—does all the things he has always wanted to do and never could.

But the story and its skilful technique cannot, of themselves, account for the unprecedented success of Plenzdorf's work. The political and literary atmosphere in which Plenzdorf wrote and in which his audience received the work contributed significantly to its success. Literature is taken much more seriously by government officials in the GDR than by their American counterparts. They believe, in fact, that literature has the power to influence the development of the society in which it is written and read. Because they are quite consciously trying to develop a socialist society, government officials in the GDR (specifically, members of the Central Committee of the Socialist Unity Party, which is *the* ruling party in the GDR) establish mandatory guidelines for the production of literature. Interestingly enough, they see no real contradiction between this and the idea of freedom of expression, in which they claim to believe.

Their official dogma is that of "socialist realism." The tenets of socialist realism were first spelled out by A. A. Zhdanov at the Congress of the Union of Soviet Writers in 1934. They are: 1) the author must describe the life of the workers, their work, and the social and technical conditions under which they are working; 2) he should attempt to educate his readers in the spirit of socialism; and 3) he should attempt to depict not objective reality, but rather reality in its revolutionary development toward the realization of the ideal of the purely socialist society. These tenets, which virtually outlaw the criticism of social or political conditions in the GDR, were adopted as official guidelines by the Central Committee of the Party in March of 1951 and have been in effect ever since.

Shortly before the publication of *The New Sufferings of Young W.*, however, something happened that gave both authors and readers new hope. In December of 1971, after the Eighth Party Congress of the Socialist Unity Party, Erich Honecker, First Secretary of the Central Committee, announced that there would be "no more taboos" for literature and art, as long as its creator "proceeds from the fixed positions of socialism." In a sense, Plenzdorf's book arrived on the market at exactly the right time—only a short time after the Honecker regime decided to loosen the reins of censorship. It was the first literary work to criticize the social conditions in the GDR and get away with it. To a certain extent, then, the tremendous popularity of Plenzdorf's work can be attributed to the fact that the hunger of the GDR reader for criticism of the society in which he lives had been abnormally intensified through years of strict government censorship, and that this was the first work containing such criticism to appear after the lifting—as it turned out, short-lived—of these controls.

The criticism that Plenzdorf allows himself is, of course, a subtle one. But it is there. It can be seen, for example, in Edgar's talk with the film writer who visits his school. Edgar complains about the movies that are written according to the dictates of the dogma of "social realism": "Then I told him what I really thought. I told him that a movie in which people are supposed to do nonstop learning could only be boring. That everyone can tell right away what they're supposed to learn, and that nobody who's spent the whole day learning wants to learn at night when he goes to the movies thinking he can have fun."

It is important to note that his criticism, like that of most citizens of the GDR, is not directed at socialism per se, for that is not only accepted, but even embraced, but rather at the authoritarian nature of the regime itself. This can be seen, for example, in the episode in which Edgar is mustering Dieter's books: "I don't know what all he had. Guaranteed, all of 'em good books. Marx, Engels, Lenin, all in neat rows. I didn't have anything against Communism and all that, the abolition of the exploitation of the world. I wasn't against that. But against everything else. That you arranged books according to their size, for example. It's the same with most of the people. They don't have anything against Communism. No half-way intelligent person can have anything against Communism these days. But they're against the other things." And these "other things" include—as Plenzdorf himself assured me in an interview I had with him in East Berlin in the fall of 1974—the so-called "achievement principle," that is, the heavy emphasis placed in the GDR on individual achievement as a measure of personal worth. This, he said, is the sense in which the controversial end of Edgar's sufferings is to be interpreted—as criticism of the "achievement principle."

Besides being a criticism of GDR society, Edgar's story is also—as the title itself indicates—a parody of that of his predecessor and in many respects model, Werther, in Johann Wolfgang von Goethe's famous book, *The Sufferings of Young Werther*. This book, first published in 1774, has been read by more people than any other work written in the German language. It is the story of a young man named Werther who, like Edgar, runs away from home, takes up residence in another city, paints, dances, falls in love, and then reports all of these things—via letters, however, not tapes—to his confidant who has stayed at home.

The relationship between Plenzdorf's *Sufferings* and Goethe's is at least two-fold. First, Edgar's story closely parallels Werther's. Even the constellation of characters is similar: Willi, Edgar's best friend, corresponds to Wilhelm, Werther's confidant; Charlie, the girl with whom Edgar falls in love, corresponds to Charlotte, Werther's beloved, and Dieter, her fiancé, corresponds to Albert, Charlotte's betrothed. Second, early in the story Edgar discovers a discarded copy of the original *Sufferings* in an outhouse. Having used the title page and epilogue as toilet paper, he then reads the book, which he finds both fascinating and alienating. In line with his own ambivalent response, he puts the book to use in two different ways. On the one hand he uses Werther's utterances to articulate his feelings when his own verbal facility proves inadequate to the task at hand, for example, in expressing his passion for "Charlie." And, on the other hand, he uses Werther's words in his own rebellion against his surroundings. Every time he feels himself threatened by the "straight" world he simply hurls a Werther quote at his would-be attacker, who is generally left baffled and thereby disarmed. In one sense, at least, Edgar and Werther are kindred spirits: both are rebels against the constraints placed on us by social convention.

But there are major differences between the two, differences that cannot be overlooked. The most important of these is that Edgar is nowhere near as "inward" as Werther. At one point in his reflections Werther says: "So it is that even the most restless rover finally longs for his native land, to find in his cottage, on the breast of his wife, in the circle of his children, in the affairs that furnish their support, the joy that he vainly sought in all the wide world." As if in direct response to this, Edgar is heard to exclaim: "I think that most people want to see the world. Whoever claims he doesn't is lying. I was always turned off when somebody claimed you can find everything in the world in Mittenberg." And this response is entirely in keeping with his reaction to Werther's "style": "Besides that style. That reeked of heart and soul and joy and tears. I can't imagine that anybody ever really talked like that, not even three centuries ago. The whole concoction consisted of nothing but letters from this impossible Werther to his buddy at home. That was probably supposed to be fantastically original or sound not-thought-out. Whoever wrote it should read Salinger some time. *That's* real, folks!"

This, then, is Edgar's real soul brother: Holden Caulfield of J. D. Salinger's *The Catcher in the Rye*. Holden is a sixteen-year-old who, having been expelled from his prep school, hides out in New York for a weekend before returning home, in order to give his parents a chance to receive and adjust to the news of his failure before he has to face them. Here the parallels abound. There are almost countless superficial ones: Both Edgar and Holden like tap dancing; they both almost go into ecstasy over the "pretty" things that girls do, like lifting their skirts before they sit down; neither of them like to be asked their age. And there are numerous more substantive ones as well: Both are rebelling against the "phoniness" of social convention; both are exaggeratedly self-conscious, and both are suffering from the feeling of alienation. Even the jargon used by Edgar is reminiscent of that used by Holden.

But, as was true in the case of Werther, the differences are as important as the similarities. Plenzdorf begins by pointing to them in little ways: Edgar had been in a boxing club for years, whereas Holden can't even make a proper fist, and Edgar doesn't even know when he last cried, whereas Holden cries several times in the course of the three days depicted in the book. But these differences only serve to point in the direction of even larger ones. One of these involves their respective attitudes toward sex. Holden fails to perform after having hired a prostitute, while Edgar claims, at least, to try "to get" every girl with whom he finds himself in the same room for more than half an hour. As regards Holden's sexual hangups, Edgar says: "That's probably the only thing that I could never understand about Salinger."

And yet there's certainly more to it than that. As is true of their respective sex lives, so too is true of their respective lives in general: Holden is simply more "hungup" than is Edgar. Whereas Holden seems to be having more trouble coping with his neurotic reactions to an oppressive society than with the society itself, Edgar seems to be finding it difficult to deal with what he views as an oppressive political system. His neuroses, if he has them, are not the essential opponent. Looming behind almost everything to which Edgar takes exception is an official policy of the Party controlling the society in which he lives.

K.P.W.

Notice in the "Berliner Zeitung," December 26:

On the night of December 24, Edgar W., a youth, was found critically injured in a garden house in Paradise II Colony in the district of Lichtenberg. According to police reports, Edgar W., who had been illegally inhabiting the condemned structure for sometime, had been carelessly tinkering with electric current.

Obituary in the "Berliner Zeitung," December 30:

On December 24 an accident ended the life of our
young colleague
Edgar Wibeau
He was a promising young man!
People's Works WIK Berlin
Local Trade-union Administration Free German Youth
Director

Obituaries in the "Volkswacht," Frankfurt/O., December 31:

A tragic accident completely unexpectedly took the life of
Edgar Wibeau
our unforgettable member.
People's Works (Communally Managed) Hydraulics of
Mittenberg
Trade School   Director   Free German Youth

Yet inconceivable to me, on December 24 my dear son
Edgar Wibeau
died as a result of a tragic accident.
Else Wibeau

"When did you last see him?"

"In September. The end of September. The night before he left."

"Didn't you ever think of a police search?"

"If anybody has the right to blame me, it's not you! Not the man who for years didn't show any more concern for his son than an occasional postcard!"

"Pardon me! That's what you wanted, wasn't it, what with my lifestyle?!"

"That's your old irony again! Not going to the police was perhaps the only right thing that I did. Even that ended up wrong. But I was simply fed up with him. He'd put me in an impossible situation at the trade school and in the factory. The son of the director, until then the best apprentice, A-average, turns out to be a rowdy! Rebels against the school! Runs away from home! I mean . . .! And then the news came from him pretty quickly and regularly. Not to me. God forbid. To his buddy, Willi. On tapes. Strange messages. So affected. Finally this Willi let me hear them; even he thought the whole thing was getting weird. Where Edgar was, in Berlin you know, he didn't want to tell me that at first. Anyway, nobody was able to get a thing out of those tapes. No matter, at least they told us one thing. That Edgar was well. That he was even working, and not wasting his time. Later a girl was mentioned, but then that broke up. She got married! As long as I had him *here* he never had anything to do with girls. But that still wasn't any reason for calling the police."

Stop, just stop! That's a lot of crap. You bet I had something to do with girls. The first time when I was fourteen. Now I can say it. You'd heard all kinds of stuff, but nothing definite. I wanted to know for sure, that's the way I am. Her name was Sylvia. She was about three years older than me. It took me exactly sixty minutes to bring her 'round. I think that's pretty fast work for my age, especially when you consider that I didn't have all my charm yet, or my distinct chin. I'm not saying that to brag, people, but just so that nobody gets a false impression of me. A year later mother enlightened me. She really exhausted herself doing it. Idiot that I am, I could have died laughing, but I played the naive, good little boy, like always. That was disgusting.

"What do you mean, he turned out to be a rowdy?!"

"He broke his teacher's toe."—"His toe?"

"He threw a heavy iron plate on his foot, a foundation plate. I was dumbfounded. I mean . . .!"

"Just like that?"

"I wasn't there, but my colleague, Flemming, told me—he's the teacher, an old and experienced teacher, dependable—that that's how it happened: Every morning he passes out the materials in the shop, these foundation plates to be filed. And the boys file them down, and while he's checking measurements he notices that Edgar's neighbor, Willi, has finished a plate, but he hasn't filed it himself. It was from the machine. In the factory the foundation plates are machine-made, of course. The boy has managed to get a hold of one, and now he presents it as his own. Naturally it's exact to the hundredth. He says to him: That's out of the machine.

Willi: Out of what machine?

Flemming: Out of the machine in plant two.

Willi: Oh, there's a machine there?! I can't be expected to know that, Sir. The last time we were in plant two was at the beginning of our apprenticeship, and then we still thought those things were egg-laying machines. And that was Edgar's cue, they'd of course arranged everything ahead of time: OK, let's assume there is a machine there. Can be. You have to ask yourself, why do we have to file down those foundation plates then? And that in our third year."

I did say that. That's true. But all off the cuff. Not a single thing was arranged. I knew what Willi and the others were planning, but I wanted to keep out of it, like always.

"Flemming: What did I tell all of you when you first started here? I told you: You get a hunk of iron! When you can make a watch from it, you've finished your apprenticeship. Not before and not after. That's his standard motto.
And Edgar: But we didn't really want to become watchmakers."

I wanted to tell Flemming that for a long time. That was not only his stupid motto, that was his whole attitude out of the Middle Ages: the era of handmade articles. Until then I'd always kept my mouth shut.

"And then right afterwards Edgar threw the foundation plate on his foot, and with such force that his toe broke. I felt like I'd been hit by a bolt of lightning. I couldn't believe it at first."

It's all true. Except for two minor details. First of all, I didn't *throw* the plate. I didn't have to. The plates themselves were heavy enough to break a stupid old toe or anything else for that matter, just with their weight. All I had to do was drop it. Which I did. And secondly, I didn't drop it *right afterwards*, but first Flemming made another little crack, specifically, he bellowed: You're the last person I would have expected that from, Wiebau!

5

By then I'd had it. I dropped the plate. Just the way that sounds: Edgar Wiebau! It's Edgar *Wibeau*! Only an idiot would say nivau instead of niveau. I mean, after all, every person has the right to be correctly called by his correct name. If you don't attach any great importance to it—that's your business. But I do attach importance to it. That'd been going on for years. Mother didn't let it bother her to be called Wiebau. She was of the opinion that that had simply come into common use, and it wouldn't have killed her, and besides, everything she'd become in the factory she'd become under the name Wiebau. And it was only natural that we'd be called Wiebau! What's the matter with the name "Wibeau"? If it'd been "Hitler" maybe, or "Himmler"! That would've been truly decent. But "Wibeau"? Wibeau is an old Huguenot name. So? In spite of all that, I suppose that really wasn't reason to drop that stupid old plate on stupid old Flemming's stupid toe. That was a real mess. Right away I knew that not a living soul would talk about our apprenticeship, only about the plate and the toe. Sometimes I would suddenly get hot and dizzy, and then I would do things, and afterwards I didn't know what I'd done. That was my Huguenot blood, or maybe my blood pressure was too high. Too high Huguenot blood pressure.

"Do you mean Edgar was afraid of the consequences, and that's why he ran away?"
"Of course. What else?"

I just want to say this: I wasn't exactly looking forward to the epilogue. "What does Edgar Wiebau (!), member of the Free German Youth, have to say about his behavior in front of Master Flemming?" People! I'd rather've ordered hamburger than to've had to season my steak with crap like: I realize . . . in the future I will . . . I hereby commit myself to . . . and so on! I had something against self-criticism, I mean: when it's public. Somehow it's degrading. I don't know if you understand me. I think that a person should be allowed to have his pride. It's the same with good examples. Somebody's always coming up to you and wants to know who you want to be like, or you have to write three essays about it every week. Can be that I have a model, but I don't make a point of telling everyone about it. Once I wrote: my best good example is Edgar Wibeau. I want to be just like what he's going to be like. Nothing more. That is: I *wanted* to write that. But I left well enough alone, people. The most that could've happened would've been that they wouldn't have graded it. Not one damn teacher dared to give me an F or something.

"Can you remember anything else?"

"You mean a fight, I suppose? We never argued. Oh, once in a fit of rage he threw himself down the stairs, because I wouldn't take him with me somewhere. He was five then, if that's what you're referring to. Just the same I suppose it's all my fault."

That is a crock of shit! It's nobody's fault, only my own. Let's be clear about that! Edgar Wibeau broke his apprenticeship and ran away from home *because he'd been planning to for a long time*. He made his way in Berlin as a painter, had his fun, had Charlotte, and almost made a great invention, *because he wanted to*.

That I passed into the Great Beyond doing it, that was really dumb. But if it consoles anyone: I didn't notice much. 380 volts are no joke, people. It went very fast. As a rule, regrets in the Great Beyond are not the usual thing. All of us here know what we're in for. That we cease to exist when you cease to think about us. My chances are probably lousy. I was too young.

"My name is Wibeau."

"Glad to meet you—Linder, Willi."

Greetings, Willi! My whole life you were my best friend, do me a favor now. Don't start grubbing around in your soul after guilt or something. Pull yourself together.

"There are supposed to be tapes from Edgar which he mentioned. Are they available? I mean, can I hear them? At your convenience?"

"Yeah. That's OK."

The tapes*:

to sum it up/wilhelm/i have made an acquaintance/which touches my heart closely—an angel—and yet i am not in a position/to tell you/in what respect she is perfect/why she is perfect/enough/she has taken possession of my whole being—end

no/i do not delude myself—i read in her black eyes true sympathy for me and for my fate—she is sacred to me—all physical desire is mute in her presence—end

enough/wilhelm/the betrothed is here—fortunate that i was not present to witness his reception—that would have rent my heart—end

he wishes me well/and i surmise/that that is Lotte's doing/for in that respect women have a fine instinct and a sound one/if they can keep two admirers on good terms with each other/that is bound to be to their advantage/however rarely it succeeds—end

that was a night—wilhelm/now i can survive anything—i shall not see her again—here i sit and gasp for air/try to calm myself/and await the morning/and the horses are ordered for sunrise

o my friends/you ask why the stream of genius so seldom bursts forth/so seldom sends its sublime floods rushing in to make your souls quake with astonishment—dear friends/why there along both banks of the river dwell the

---

* All of the tape passages are taken from *The Sufferings of Young Werther*, translated from the German of Johann Wolfgang von Goethe by Bayard Quincy Morgan (Ungar, 1957).

placid conservatives/whose summer houses/tulip beds and cabbage fields would be ruined/and who consequently manage to avert betimes with dams and drainage ditches any future threat—all this/wilhelm/forces me into silence—i return into myself and find a world—end

and for all this you are to blame/who talked me into undergoing this yoke and prated so much about activity—activity—i have petitioned the court for my dismissal—feed this to my mother in a sweet syrup—end

"Understand it?"

"No. Nothing."

Of course you can't. Nobody can, I'd guess. I got it from an old book, a paperback. A Reclam paperback. I'm not even sure what it was called. The stupid old cover got flushed down the stupid old john in Willi's garden house. The whole thing was written in this impossible style.

"Sometimes I think—a code."

"It makes too much sense for a code. But then on the other hand it doesn't sound thought-out either."

"You could never tell about Ed. He came up with some really weird stuff. Whole songs, for example. Words *and* music! There wasn't a musical instrument that he couldn't learn to play in two days. Or at least in a week. He was able to make calculators out of cardboard that still work today. But most of the time we painted."

"Edgar painted? What kind of pictures were they?"

"Always GIN A2."*

"I mean: what kinds of motifs? Or can I see some of them?"

"Impossible. He had them all with him. And you

---

* GIN (German Industrial Norms) is an abbreviation used by the GDR government. It means: "meeting government standards" or "satisfactory." A2 means: "second class."

can hardly talk about motifs. We always painted abstract. One was called physics. Another: chemistry. Or: the brain of a mathematician. It was just that his mother was against it. Ed should've had a "decent job" first. That used to really tick Ed off, if you're interested. But he got maddest when he found out that she, his mother, had gotten a card from his progenitor . . . I mean: his father . . . I mean: you, and had hidden it from him. That happened every once in a while. Then he was really ticked.

That's true. I thought that really stunk. After all, there was such a thing as the privacy of letters, and the cards were plainly addressed to me. To Mr. Edgar Wibeau, the stupid old Huguenot. Any idiot could have seen that I wasn't supposed to know anything about my progenitor, the slob who drank and chased after women. The bad man from Mittenberg. Him with his paintings that nobody could understand, which was always the paintings' fault of course.

"And you believe that that's why he ran away?"

"I don't know . . . Anyway, what most people think, that Ed ran away 'cause of this thing with Flemming, that's pure bullshit. Why he did that, I don't really know that either. Ed had it easy. He was tops in all his classes, without hitting the books. And he never got himself involved in anything. There was always a lot of trouble there. People called him "mama's boy." Not to his face, of course. Ed didn't let it get to him. Or maybe he didn't hear it. For example, that business with the mini-skirts. The broads, I mean: the girls in our class, they just couldn't stop themselves from showing up in the shop in mini-skirts, on the job. In order to give the teachers a thrill. It had already been forbidden umpteen times. That really ticked us off, so we, us guys, showed up at work one morning with mini-skirts. That was really quite a spectacle. Ed didn't take part. That was probably too silly for him.

Sorry. I just didn't have anything against short skirts. You drag yourself completely zonked out of bed in the morning, see a woman through the window, and already you begin to feel better. Beyond that, as far as I'm concerned anyone can wear what they please. Just the same, I thought the whole thing was a good joke. Could have been my own idea. The only reason I stay'd out of it was that I didn't want to cause any trouble for mother. That was really my big mistake: I never wanted to cause any trouble for mother. In fact, I'd gotten into the habit of never causing any trouble for anybody. Do that, and you never have any fun. After a while it really begins to bug you. I don't know if you know what I mean. That brings us to the subject of why I split. I was just sick of running around as living proof that you can raise a child very well without a father. That was what I was supposed to be. One day I had the crazy idea, what would've happened if I'd suddenly croaked, smallpox or something. I mean, what would I have gotten out of life. I just couldn't stop thinking about it.

"If you ask me—Ed went away because he wanted to be a painter. That was the reason. It's just too bad that they turned him down at the art school in Berlin."
"Why?"
"Ed said: untalented. No imagination. He was really ticked."

Was I ever! But the *fact* was that my collected works weren't worth a damn. Why do you think we always painted abstract? Because, idiot that I am, I could never in my whole life have painted something real so that you would have recognized it, a stupid old dog or something. I guess that the whole thing with painting was genuine insanity on my part.

11

Even so, that wasn't a bad show, where I came charging into this art school and right into this professor's room and slammed my collected works down on the table right in front of him.

First he asked: How long have you been doing that?

I: Don't know! A long time.

I wasn't looking at him.

He: Do you have a job?

I: Not that I know of. Why should I?

He should have at least thrown me out at that point. But the man was tough. He stuck with it.

He: Is there any order to this? Which one's last, which one's first?

He was referring to my exhibit on the table.

I: The earlier works are on the left.

The early works! Man! Did I pull that off well. That was a low blow.

He: How old are you?

This guy was really tough!

I mumbled: Nineteen!

I don't know if he believed me.

He: Imagination you've got. There's no question there, none at all, and you can draw too. If you had a job, I'd say: draftsman.

I began to pack up my stuff.

He: I could be mistaken. Leave your things here for a few days. It's a known fact that four or even six eyes see more than two.

I packed up. Stubborn. There never was a more unrecognized genius than me.

"You stayed in Berlin in spite of that."

"Ed—not me. I couldn't. But I encouraged him. Theoretically that was right too. After all, there's no better place than Berlin to go underground and then make a name for yourself. I mean, I didn't tell him to stay here or anything. You couldn't get anywhere with Ed like that. We had a garden house in Berlin. We moved from Berlin when my father got transferred here. We didn't get rid of the garden house, they were supposed to put up new houses. In any case I had the key. The place was still in pretty good shape. We looked it over, and I talked the idea down the whole time. The roof was caving in. Someone had swiped the stupid old slipcover off the sofa. Our old furniture was still there, like that always happens. And the house was about to be torn down, because of the new housing project. Ed was getting more and more determined. He unpacked his things. His things! Actually he didn't have any more than the pictures, only the clothes on his back. His burlap jacket that he'd sewn together himself, with copper wire, and his old jeans.

Naturally jeans! Or can you imagine a life without jeans? Jeans are the greatest pants in the world. For jeans I'd give up all of the synthetic rags in Jumo* that always look squeaky clean. For jeans I would give up everything, except maybe for the *finest thing*. And except for music. I don't mean just an old Händelsohn Bacholdy, I mean genuine music, people. I didn't have anything against Bacholdy or the others, but they didn't exactly sweep me off my feet. Of course I mean real jeans. There's a whole pile of junk that just pretends to be jeans. If that's all I could get I'd rather not have any at all. Real jeans, for example, don't have a zipper in front. There is only one kind of real jeans. A real jeans wearer knows what I mean. That doesn't mean that everyone who wears real jeans is a real jeans wearer. Most of them don't even know what they're wearing. It always killed me when I saw some twenty-five-year-old fogy with jeans on that he's forced up over his bloated thighs and then belted up tight at the waist. Jeans are supposed to be hip pants, I mean

* A large department store in East Berlin.

they're pants that will slip down off your hips if you don't buy them small enough, and they stay up by friction. You naturally can't have fat hips and certainly not a fat ass, because otherwise they won't snap together. People over twenty-five are too dense to grasp that. That is, if they're card-carrying Communists and beat their wives. I mean, jeans are an attitude and not just pants. Sometimes I think that people shouldn't be allowed to get older than seventeen—or eighteen. After that they get a job or go to college or join the army and then there's no reasoning with them anymore. At least I haven't known any. Maybe nobody understands me. Then you start wearing jeans that you don't any more have a right to. It's also great when you're retired and then wear jeans, with a belly and suspenders. That's also great. But I haven't known any, except Zaremba. Zaremba was great. He could've worn some, if he'd wanted to, and it wouldn't have bothered anybody.

"Edgar even wanted me to stay. 'We'll make it' he said. But that wasn't planned, and besides, I couldn't. Ed could, I couldn't. I wanted to, but I couldn't.

Then Ed said: When you get home tell 'em I'm living, and that's all. That was the last thing he said. Then I left."

You're OK, Willi. You can stay that way. You're a stubborn bastard. I'm pleased with you. If I had written a will I'd have made you my sole inheritor. Maybe I've always underestimated you. That was really sly, the way you talked me into the garden house. But I wasn't being honest with you either when I said you should stay. I mean, I was being honest. We'd have gotten along good together. But I wasn't being really honest. When somebody has never in his whole life had a chance to be really alone and suddenly *gets* the chance, then it can be really hard to be honest. I hope you didn't notice. If you did, forget it. Anyway, as soon as you left I got into a really crazy mood. First I just wanted to crash, automatically. My time had come. Then I began to see that from now on I could do anything I felt like. That nobody could tell me what to do anymore. That I didn't have to wash my hands before dinner anymore if I didn't want to. I really should have eaten, but I wasn't *that* hungry. So I scattered all my rags and other crap around the room as unsystematically as possible. The socks on the table. That was the crowning glory. Then I grabbed the microphone, flicked on the recorder, and began one of my private broadcasts: Ladies and gentlemen! Boys and girls! Just and unjust! Relax! Shoo your little brothers and sisters off to the movies! Lock your parents in the pantry! Here is your Eddie again, the irrepressible . . .

I began with my blue jeans song, which I had written three years ago and which got better every year.

Oh, Bluejeans
White Jeans?—No
Black Jeans?—No
Blue Jeans, oh
Oh, Bluejeans, yeah

Oh, Bluejeans
Old Jeans?—No
New Jeans?—No
Blue Jeans, oh
Oh, Bluejeans, yeah

Maybe you can imagine it. All of that in this very rich sound, in *his* style. Some people think that *he's* dead. That's bullshit. Satchmo can't be killed, because Jazz can't be killed. I don't think that I'd ever before done a better job with this song. Afterwards I felt like Robinson Crusoe and Satchmo at the same time. Robinson Satchmo. I, idiot that I am, I pinned all my collected works up on the wall. Just the same, at last everybody could tell immediately: Here lives the unrecognized genius, Edgar Wibeau. Maybe I was an idiot, people, but I was really high. I didn't know what to do first. Actually I wanted to go right downtown and check out Berlin, all the nightlife and everything and the Huguenot museum. I probably already said that I'm a Huguenot on my father's side. I was positive that I'd be able to find traces of the Wibeau family in Berlin. I think, idiot that I am, that I was hoping that maybe they'd be noblemen. Edgar de Wibeau and everything. But I told myself that no museum would be open so late. Besides that, I didn't know where it was.

I analyzed myself quickly and decided that I really wanted to read, at least until morning. Then I wanted to crash until noon and then see what was going on in Berlin. That's what I wanted to do everyday: sleep until noon and then live until midnight. I never really came alive until noon anyway. My problem was only that I didn't have any stuff— I hope that nobody thinks I mean hash or opium. I didn't have anything against hash. Of course I'd never tried any. But I think that I, idiot that I am, would've been idiotic enough to have taken some if I'd been able to get hold of some somewhere. Out of pure curiosity. Old Willi and I had once collected banana skins for a half a year and dried them. That's supposed to be as good as hash. I didn't notice a damn thing, except my spit got thick and glued my whole throat together. We lay on the carpet, turned the recorder on, and smoked these skins. When nothing happened I started to roll my eyes around in my head and to laugh ecstatically and to spin around like maniac as if I was somehow high. When old Willi saw that he started to do the same thing, but I'm convinced that it wasn't doing any more to him than it was to me. By the way, I never tried that banana stuff or any of that other crap again, ever! What I meant was, I didn't have any stuff to read. Or did you think I'd dragged my books along with me? Not even my favorites. I thought, I don't want to drag all that crap from my childhood around with me. Besides, I practically memorized those two books. My opinion about books is that nobody can read all of them, not even all the good ones. Consequently, I concentrated on just two.

Anyway, my opinion is that almost *all* books are in each book. I don't know if you understand me. I mean, in order to write a book you've got to have already read a couple a thousand others. At least I can't imagine it any other way. Say, three thousand. And each one of those was written by somebody who'd read three thousand himself. Nobody knows how many books there are. But by simple calculation there are at least . . . umpteen billion times two. I thought that that was enough. My two favorite books were: Robinson Crusoe. I know one of you's going to smirk. Never in my life would I have admitted that. The other was by this Salinger guy. I got my hands on it by pure accident. No one had even heard of it. I mean, no one had recommended it to me or anything. That's just as well. Then I wouldn't have touched it. My experience with recommended books was extremely lousy. I, idiot that I am, I was so stupid that I would think a recommended book was dumb, even when it was good. Even so, I still get pale when I think that I might never've gotten a hold of this book. This Salinger is a great guy. How he creeps around in New York in the rain and can't come home 'cause he's run away from school where they wanted to kick him out anyway, that really got to me. If I'd known his address I'd have written him, he should come over here. He must have been exactly my age. Mittenberg was of course a hole compared to New York, but he would've recovered magnificently over here. Above all, we'd have gotten rid of his dumb sexual problems for him. That's probably the only thing that I could never understand about Salinger. Probably that's easy to say if you've never had sexual problems. I can only say, if you've got problems like that, you should get yourself a girl friend. I don't mean just any old girl friend. Never that. But if you notice, for example, that you both laugh about the same things. That's always a good sign, people. I could've told Salinger right away about at least two in Mittenberg who would have laughed about the same things as him. And if not, then we'd have gotten them to.

If I'd wanted to I could have plopped myself down and

17

could have read the whole book from cover to cover or Crusoe for that matter. I mean, I could have read them in my head. That was always my technique at home when I didn't want to cause a certain Mrs. Wibeau any trouble. But after all, I didn't have to resort to that anymore. I started to scour Willi's garden house for books. It almost blew my mind. His parents must have suddenly gotten affluent. They'd stored the complete furnishings for a four-room apartment here with everything that goes with it. But not one damn book, not even a piece of newspaper. No paper at all, in fact. Not even in that hole of a kitchen. Complete furnishings, but not one book. Willi's folks must've really clung to their books. Suddenly I felt sick. The yard was as dark as a dungeon. I ran so fast I practically cracked my stupid old skull open on the pump and then on the trees before I found the outhouse. Actually, I only wanted to take a leak, but like always the rumor spread itself through both intestines. That had always been a real pain in my life. I've never been able to keep the two affairs apart. If I had to take a leak, then I always had to take a shit, there was no stopping it. And no paper, people. I fumbled around in the john like a madman. And that's how I got my hands on this famous book, this paperback. It was too dark to recognize anything. First I sacrificed the cover, then the title page, and then the last few pages, where, according to my experience, the epilogue is located, which nobody ever reads anyway. When I got out into the light again I found out that my work had in fact been perfect. Beforehand I paused for a moment of silence. After all, I had just gotten rid of the last remains of Mittenberg. After two pages I threw the turkey into the corner. People, absolutely nobody would have read that trash. With all good intentions. Five minutes later I had the turkey in my hands again. Either I was going to read until morning or not at all. That's the way I am. Three hours later I had it behind me.

Was I ticked! The guy in the book, Werther, he was called, commits suicide in the end. Just turns in his cards. Blows his stupid old brains out because he can't get the woman he wants and really feels sorry for himself doing it. If he wasn't completely retarded he had to see that she, this Charlotte, was only waiting for him to *do* something. I mean, when I'm alone in a room with a woman, and I know that nobody's coming in for the next half hour or so, people, then I try *everything*. Can be that I'll get slapped a few in the process. So what? Still better than to let an opportunity slip by. Besides, getting slapped is involved in only two out of ten cases at the most. That's a fact. And this Werther was alone with her hundreds of times. In this park, for example. And what's he do? He looks on peacefully while she gets married. And then he kills himself. He was beyond help.

I only really felt sorry for the woman. There she was stuck with her husband, that sissy. Werther should at least have thought of her. OK, let's suppose that he really couldn't have moved in on her. That was no reason to blow his brains out. After all, he did have a horse! I'd have been off in the woods in no time. There was enough of them then. Thousand to one he'd have found at least a million friends. For example, Thomas Münzer* or someone. That just wasn't real. Pure bullshit. Besides that style. That reeked of heart and soul and joy and tears. I can't imagine that anybody ever really talked like that, not even three centuries ago. The whole concoction consisted of nothing but letters from this impossible Werther to his buddy at home. That was probably supposed to be fantastically original or sound not thought-out. Whoever wrote it should read Salinger sometime. *That's* real, folks.

I can only tell you, you've got to read it, if you can just get your hands on it. Swipe it if you have to, wherever you can find it, and don't give it back. Check it out and don't return it. Just say you've lost it. That'll cost you five marks, so what? Don't let the title fool you. I admit it doesn't really do

* Religious revolutionary at the time of Martin Luther. Known for his "Christian communism."

anything for you. Maybe it's badly translated or something, but who cares? Or see the movie. That is, I don't exactly know if there is a movie of it. That's the way it was with Robinson. I could picture everything to myself, every scene. I don't know if you know what I mean. You can envision everything like it would be in the movie, and then you would find out there isn't any movie. But if there really isn't any Salinger film I can only advise every producer to shoot one. He's got it made. I don't know if I would have gone myself. I think it would have scared me to have my own film destroyed. I was never a big movie fan. If it wasn't Chaplin or something like that, these overdone bowler hat films where they make the pigs in those idiotic jungle hats look like asses, you couldn't force me into the theater. Or *To Sir With Love* with Sidney Poitier, maybe somebody's seen that one. I could've seen that one every day. I'm not talking about those required films for history class of course. You *have* to go to those. They were in the curriculum. By the way, I liked going to those. You get in an hour what it would take you forever and three days to read in the history book. I've always thought that was practical. I'd like just once to have talked to somebody who makes those films. I'd have said to him: Keep up the good work. I think that people like that should be encouraged. They save you a lot of time. I once knew a guy from the movies. He wasn't a producer, but he did write the scripts, even though I don't think they were the ones for the history films.

He just grinned when I told him what I thought about it. I couldn't make it clear to him that I was serious. I met him one day at the trade school when they dragged us off to one of those films, that he'd supplied the script for. Afterwards: discussion with the creators. But not everyone who wanted to—only the best, the model students—as a reward. The whole show took place during class time. And Edgar Wibeau was naturally right up there at the front, this intelligent, educated, disciplined boy. Our finest specimen.

And all the other finest specimens from the other grades, two from each grade.

The film took place in the present. I don't want to make a big deal out of it. Naturally I'd never have gone voluntarily, unless of course the Medium Soft had done the music for it. I assume they wanted to get into the film business. It was about this dude who'd just gotten out of the clink and wanted to start a new life. Until then he'd always been a little suspect, I mean politically, and the cooler hadn't done a lot to change that. His crime was assault and battery. He'd once attacked a veteran because he'd gotten him mad in a conversation about too loud and piercing music. Right out of jail he went to the hospital, because of jaundice, I guess. Anyway, nobody was allowed to visit him. He didn't know anybody anyway. But in the hospital there was this propagandist or whatever that was supposed to be in the same room with him. At least he talked like it. As soon as I saw that I knew right away what was coming. The man would talk to him until he realized his mistakes, and then they would make him conform beautifully. And that's the way it really happened. He joined a splendid work crew with a splendid foreman, met a splendid co-ed, whose parents were against it at first, but they accepted it splendidly when they saw what a splendid boy he'd become, and finally he was allowed to join the army. I don't know who's seen this splendid film, people. The only thing that still interested me, besides the music, was the hero's brother. He dragged him with him everywhere he went, because he was supposed to conform too. They were always looking for this propagandist. That's supposed to be touching or something. The brother let himself be dragged along, he even got a kick out of all the traveling, and he even got to like this splendid co-ed, and she him, and one time I thought, just one word and he'll bring her around, if he wants to. Anyway, from that moment on I started to like her. He cooperated with everything, but he didn't conform for a long time. He wanted to be a clown in the circus,

21

and he wouldn't let himself be talked out of it. They said he just wanted to fool around instead of getting a steady job. A steady job, people, I'd heard that line before! Naturally he wanted to join the circus because there he could see the world, among other things, or at least part of it. What's wrong with that? I understood him completely. I couldn't see why that should be bad. I think that most people want to see the world. Whoever claims he doesn't is lying. I was always turned off when somebody claimed you can find everything in the world in Mittenberg. And this brother was turned off, too.

This guy that wrote it started to interest me. I watched him the whole time we sat in the classroom and talked about how great we thought the film was and everything that we could learn from it. First all the teachers and the educators who were there told us what we could learn from it and then we told them what we'd learned from it. The man didn't say anything the whole time. He looked as if this whole show with model students really bored him. Then there was a tour for the film producers through all of our classrooms and everything. At the first opportunity we threw ourselves at the man, me and Old Willi. We hung on to him and stayed behind with him. I had the feeling he was thankful for that, at least at first. Then I told him what I really thought. I told him that a movie in which people are supposed to do nonstop learning could only be boring. That everyone can tell right away what they're supposed to learn, and that nobody who's spent the whole day learning wants to learn at night when he goes to the movies thinking he can have fun. He said that he'd always thought that himself, but that it had to be that way. I advised him just to give it up and to start making those history films where everybody knows from the start that they're not supposed to have fun. Then he saw to it that he caught up with his group which was getting a lecture from Flemming on our outstanding educational facilities. We let him go. Anyhow, I had the feeling that he was raging on the inside about something that had happened that day or maybe just things in general. I'm only sorry that I didn't have his address. Maybe he was in Berlin, then I could have visited him, and he couldn't have taken off.

"Do the Schmidts live here?"

"Who'd you want to see?"

"Mrs. Schmidt."

"That's me. You're in luck."

"Good. My name is Wibeau. Edgar's father."

"How'd you find me?"

"It wasn't easy."

"I mean, how'd you know about me?"

"From the tapes. Edgar'd sent tapes to Mittenberg, like letters."

"I didn't know anything about that. And there's something about me on them?"

"Only a little. That your name is Charlotte, and that you're married. And that you have black eyes."

Easy, Charlie. I didn't say anything. Not one word.

"What do you mean, Charlotte? My name isn't Charlotte."

"I didn't know. Why are you crying? Please don't cry."

Stop howling, Charlie. Knock it off! That's no reason to howl. I got the name from that dumb book.

"I'm sorry, but Edgar was an idiot. Edgar was a stubborn, obstinate idiot. There was no way to help me. Excuse me."

That's right. I was an idiot. Man, was I ever. But stop howling. I don't think anybody can imagine what an idiot I was.

"Actually I came to see if you maybe had a picture he'd made."

"Edgar couldn't paint at all. That was also one of his idiocies. Everyone knew it, but he just wouldn't listen. And if you said it to him right to his face he'd babble some nonsense that nobody could understand. Probably not even himself."

That's when you were at your best, Charlie, when you'd really gotten yourself worked up. But that everybody could see right away that I couldn't paint is not exactly correct. I mean, you might have seen it, but I was really good at acting as if I could. That's really one of the greatest tricks, people. It doesn't matter whether or not you can do something, the main thing is to act as if you can. Then it works. At least with painting and art and that stuff. A pair of pliers is good if it grips. But a picture or something like that? Nobody really knows whether it's good or not.

"It started already on the first day. Our kindergarten had a playground in the housing project, with a sandbox, swings, and a teeter-totter. In the summer we spent the whole day there when we could. Now everything's been torn up. The children always charged straight from the sandbox onto the jungle gym and into the bushes. They were on the neighboring lot, but it practically belonged to us. The fence had disappeared a long time before, and we hadn't seen anybody there for ages. The whole subdivision was going to be torn down. Suddenly I saw someone coming out of the garden house, a guy, unkempt and really degenerate looking. Right away I called the children to me."

That was me. People, was I ever zonked. I was really outstandingly zonked. I didn't see anything. I dragged myself to the privy and from there to the pump. But I just couldn't touch the pump water. I could have drunk an ocean, but the pump water would have killed me. I don't know if you can understand it. I'd just plain woken up too early. Charlie's brats had woken me with their screaming.

"That was Edgar?"

"That was Edgar. I immediately forbade the children to go there again. But you know how children are—five minutes later they were all gone. I called them, and then I saw: there they were, with Edgar. Edgar sat behind his garden house with his painting gear, and they were all behind him, dead silent."

That's true. I was never a child lover. I didn't have anything against children, but I was never a child lover. They can really bug you in the long run, at least me, or men in general. Or did you ever hear of a *male* kindergarten teacher? It's just that it always really pissed me off when somebody was supposed to be a degenerate or immoral or something because he had long hair, unpressed pants, didn't get up at five, and didn't wash himself down with pump water first thing in the morning and didn't know what income bracket he'd be in when he got to be fifty. So I fished out all my painting gear and planted myself behind the garden house and started to take my bearings with a pencil like all painters are supposed to do. And five minutes later Charlie's brats were all behind me in full strength.

"What was he painting?"

"Actually, nothing. Lines. The children wanted to know too."

Edgar said: We'll see. Maybe a tree?

Instantly: What do you mean, maybe? Don't you know what you're going to paint?

And Edgar: That all depends on what the morning holds for me. How can you know ahead of time? First of all a painter has to loosen himself up. Otherwise the tree that he wants to paint will be too stiff.

25

They enjoyed themselves. Edgar knew how to get along with children, but he certainly couldn't paint. I could tell that right away. I'm kind of interested in painting."

Stop it, Charlie! They enjoyed themselves all right, but the joke about the tree was yours. I was still thinking: That's the way it always is. You're having fun and then the kindergarten teacher comes along and gives you a serious explanation. And then I turned around and looked at you. I thought I'd been hit by a truck. I had underestimated you. That was plain irony. I think that the whole thing, this tug of war of ours, began right there. Both of us wanted to pull the other one over the line. Charlie wanted to prove to me that I couldn't paint worth a damn, and that I was just an overgrown child, that I couldn't live like that and that I needed help. And I wanted to prove the opposite to her. That I was an unrecognized genius, that I could live my own life, that I didn't need any help, and above all, that I was anything but a child. Besides, from the beginning I wanted to have her. To lay her, no matter what happened, but to have her too. I don't know if you know what I mean, people.

"You mean, he couldn't draw realistically? He couldn't even sketch?"

"He couldn't draw at all. It was also clear to me why he pretended he could: he wanted people to think he was an unrecognized genius. I've just never understood why. That was a real tick with him. I got the idea of bringing him to our kindergarten and letting him paint on one of the walls. He couldn't have hurt anything. Our school was going to be torn down. The principal didn't have anything against it. I thought Edgar would try to get out of it. But he came. It's just that he was so shrewd. Excuse me, but he was really shrewd. He just gave each of the children a paintbrush and let them all paint anything they wanted. I knew right away what would happen. In half an hour there was the most beautiful fresco on the wall. And Edgar hadn't made a single brush stroke or at least as good as none."

The thing came off fantastically, I knew it would. I knew that nothing could happen. Children can really bore you but they can paint so it'll just knock you over. If I wanted to look at pictures I'd rather go to a kindergarten than a stupid old museum. Besides, they just love to smear up the whole wall.

The teacher's aides were astounded. They thought it was just fantastic, what their kids had painted. I thought it was pretty good myself. It really knocked me right over, the way kids can paint. And Charlie couldn't do anything about it. The others delegated her to bring me some lunch. They'd probably noticed that Charlie could mean something to me. They'd have had to've been stupid not to. I just sat there watching her starry-eyed the whole time. I don't mean I really stared at her like a wild-eyed kid the whole time. Not that, people! I didn't have especially impressive optical organs in my stupid old Huguenot skull. They're regular pig slits in comparison with Charlie's headlights. But brown. Brown is dynamite, serious.

Back at my kolkhoz* I got the best idea of my life. At least it's gotten me a lot of laughs. It was really dynamite. I got my hands on this book again, this paperback. Automatically I started to read it again. I had the time, and above all I had the *idea*. I shot into my room, flipped on my recorder, and dictated to Willi:

I'd gotten that directly out of the book, even the Wilhelm. To sum it up, Wilhelm, I have made an acquaintance which touches my heart closely . . . An angel . . . And yet I am not in a position to tell you in what respect she is perfect, why she is perfect; enough! she has taken possession of my whole being. End.

* Russian word for collective farm. Here it means as much as "my place."

That's how I first got onto the *idea*. I got the tape off to the post office right away. I owed Willi a letter anyway. It was only too bad that I couldn't see Willi fall over. He must've keeled over. He must've gotten cramps. He probably rolled his eyes around in his head and fell out of his chair.

"Could I see this mural?"

"Unfortunately not. The building has been torn down. We're in a new building now.

I do have one of Edgar's pictures. But there's nothing to see in it. It's a silhouette. I told you: he wouldn't believe me. That was a day later. I came to him. We wanted to pay him a fee. Then I got the idea of asking him to draw a picture of me, this time without help. We were alone, of course. What'd he do? This silhouette. Anybody can do that. But I saw his other pictures in his garden house. I can't describe them. They were just jumbled confusion. That was probably supposed to be abstract. But it was only jumbled! Really as a matter of fact, everything was always jumbled at his place. I don't mean dirty, but jumbled and sloppy as can be."

You're a hundred percent correct, Charlie. Jumbled and sloppy and everything, just like you say. At first I thought I'd been run over by a bus, people, with Charlie standing there in my room. Luckily it was the afternoon and I was pretty much awake. But that with the money was clear to me from the start. Because of a fee! That was Charlie's own money and beyond that an excuse. She just couldn't get her mind off me.

At first I acted modest. I said: What for? I didn't even raise a finger.

And Charlie: Just the same!—Without your supervision it would never have worked.

Then I said it right to her face: That's your own money, and you know it. A fee? No way!

Then she got an idea: OK. But I'll get it back again. Just

has to be approved from upstairs. I thought you could use it.

I still had some money, but I definitely could've used it. People, you can always use money. But I didn't take it anyway. I knew what it would mean. It would mean she thought I was a bum or something. I didn't do her that favor. When that was settled she actually should've left. But that isn't the way Charlie was. That just wasn't her. Her skull was at least as thick as mine. I mean head. With women you should probably say head.

Besides, the whole time I was telling her that she really could mean something to me. I mean, naturally I didn't say it in so many words. Actually I didn't say anything at all. But she still noticed, I think. And then she started with her idea about my painting a picture of her. Supposedly just for fun. And I was supposed to believe that! Charlie was talented maybe, but she was a lousy actress. That didn't suit her. For about three seconds I looked pretty worried, until I got the idea with the candle. I put Charlie on a stupid old stool, darkened the room, pinned a hunk of paper on the wall and started twisting her head around in the light. Naturally I could have moved the stupid old candle around instead, but I wasn't that dumb. I took a hold of her whole chin and turned her head. Charlie swallowed hard, but she went along with it. I used every trick I could think of: the painter and his model. Supposedly there's nothing erotic in that, but I think that's bullshit. That's probably something the painters dreamed up so their models won't all run away. In my case, something clicked, and in Charlie's too, at least. But she didn't have a chance! She just wouldn't take her eyes off me. These headlights of hers. I was just about to try *everything*. But I analyzed myself and decided that I didn't want *everything*. I mean I did, but just not right away. I don't know if you understand me, people. For the first time in my life I wanted to wait with that. Besides, I probably would have gotten slapped. For sure. Then I still would have gotten slapped. I just kept my cool and made this silhouette of her.

When I was done she started right in: give it to me! For my fiancé. He's in the army.

If one of you thinks that that really got on my nerves or something, that about the fiancé, he's wrong, people. Being engaged is a long way from being married. Anyway, at least Charlie had figured out what the name of the game was. *That* was exactly it! She started to take me seriously. I'd heard that one before. Fiancés always pop up when it starts to get too serious. Naturally I didn't give her the silhouette. I mumbled something like: It's still too rough . . . Needs some life. As if you could put life into it. Especially not without her eyes. And Charlie's eyes were regular headlights, or did I already say that? I just had to keep it. I wanted to varnish it and keep it for myself. That really got her angry. She dug in her heels and told me to my face: You can't paint at all, at least not correctly. That's all just an excuse for something. You're also not from Berlin, anyone can see that. You don't have a real job, and anyway you don't earn any money painting, how you do otherwise, I don't know. She'd really gotten herself wound up.

But I wasn't lazy either: I thought for a minute and blurted out the following:

Uniformity marks the human race. Most of them spend the greater part of their time in working for a living, and the scanty freedom that is left to them burdens them so that they seek every means of getting rid of it.

Charlie didn't say a thing. She probably hadn't understood a word of it. Which isn't surprising, what with that style. Naturally I had gotten it from that book. I don't know if I told you that I can memorize things from books fantastically. That was a real pain in my life. It had its advantages, of course, in school for example. I mean every teacher is satisfied when he hears a passage from a book he knows. I couldn't blame them. They don't need to check if it's all right, like they do with their own words. And they were all satisfied.

"Am I mistaken, or did you have a fight with him?"

"We didn't fight. I told him to his face that I thought he was lazy. I almost thought maybe he was involved in something crooked. He must have gotten money somehow. I'm sorry. I know that's nonsense, but you really couldn't figure him out."

"And him? Edgar?"

"Edgar did what he always did in such cases, only that day was the first time for me: He talked rubbish. I can't think of anything else to call it. You couldn't even remember it. The stuff was really that insane. Maybe it had some meaning, but it was really queer. And it wasn't his own. Probably from the Bible, that's what I think sometimes. He just wanted to flabbergast you with it, that's all."

Maybe I shouldn't have even tried that joke on Charlie. Even so, her reaction was priceless.

Then she asked me: How old are you actually? My age! She just wanted to show me that she could have been my mother. She couldn't have been more than two years older than me. I said: three thousand seven hundred and sixty-seven years old, or is it seventy-six? I always confuse those two. Then she left. I admit that this question always bugged me. Even from a woman who could have meant something to me. It always forced you to lie. I mean, you can't help your age. And if you're more mature than the average seventeen-year-old it's pretty dumb to tell the truth, if you want to be taken seriously. If you want to see a movie and you've got to be eighteen, you don't stand there and scream: I'm only seventeen, do you? By the way, I used to go to the movies quite a bit. At least that was better than sitting at home with Mother Wibeau in front of the boob tube.

The first thing I did when Charlie'd left: I stuck in a new tape and reported to Willi:

No, I do not delude myself! I read in her black eyes

true sympathy for me, and for my fate. She is sacred to me. All physical desire is mute in her presence. End.

People! Was that ever a crock. Especially that stuff about desire. But on the other hand, it wasn't really so dumb. I just couldn't come to grips with that language. Sacred! I could hardly wait to see what Willi would do with that one.

After that I really wanted to hear some music. I shoved in the cassette with all the records by the Medium Soft on it and started to move. Slowly at first. I knew that I had time. The tape lasted at least fifty minutes. I had just about everything those guys did. They played so it just knocks you over. I couldn't dance very well, at least not in public. I mean, still at least three times as good as anybody else. But I really only got warmed up between my own four walls. Outside the eternal breaks in the music always messed me up. You're just beginning to get started and bang—they cut. That always made me sick. This music has to be played nonstop, preferably with two bands. Otherwise no one can get into proper form. The Negroes know that. I mean the Blacks. You should say Blacks. It's just, where else could you find bands like the Medium Soft? You should just be glad that they existed. Especially the organist. In my opinion they only could have gotten him from a seminary, a heretic or something. I'd almost busted my ass trying to round up all these guys' albums. They were dynamite. Fifteen minutes and I was really high for the second time in the last few days. Usually I only accomplished that once a year at the most. I was beginning to see that coming to Berlin was the perfect thing for me. If for no other reason, then because of Charlie. Man, was I high! I don't know if you know what I mean. If I could have I'd have invited all of you. I had at least three hundred and sixty minutes of music in the cassettes. I believe that I'm a really talented dancer. Edgar Wibeau, the great rhythmist, equally great in Beat and Soul. I could also tap dance. I'd nailed taps on an old pair of gym shoes. It was fantastic, serious. And if my cassettes hadn't held out we'd have gone to the "Eisenbahner" or even better to the "Grosse Melodie" where the Medium Soft played or the SOK or Petrowski or Old Lenz, depending on who was there. We always went on Mondays. Or does one of you think maybe I didn't know where to go in Berlin for real music? After *one* week I knew that. I don't think there was much in Berlin I missed. I was like in one constant stream of music. Maybe you can understand me. I'd been like starving. I'd estimate that there wasn't one decent group that had any idea of what music is in a two hundred kilometer radius of Mittenberg. Old Lenz and Uschi Brüning! Whenever that woman started I just about died. I don't think she's any worse than Ella Fitzgerald or anybody else for that matter. I'd have given her everything, the way she'd stand up there with her huge glasses and practice with the group. And the way she'd communicate with the leader with just a look, that must have been transmigration of souls or something. And the way she'd thank him with just a look when he let her start in. I could've cried every time. He'd hold her back until she just couldn't stand it anymore, and then he'd let her start in, and then she'd always thank him with this smile, and I'd just about go out of my head. Could be that it was completely different with Lenz. Just the same, the "Grosse Melodie," it was a kind of paradise for me, like heaven. I don't think that I lived on much besides milk and music then.

At first my only problem at the "Grosse Melodie" was that I didn't have long hair. I really looked out of place. As a genuine model student in Mittenberg I naturally wasn't even allowed to have a shag, much less *long* hair. I don't know if you can imagine what a pain that was. I cringed when I saw the others with their manes, naturally only on the inside. Otherwise I claimed that long hair didn't mean anything to me 'cause as long as everybody had it it didn't take any courage. Besides, having long hair was a nonstop hassle. Just the way people looked at it. I don't know if you know what I mean, people. That face that they make when they tell you that you can't have long hair in the shop or someplace else, for safety reasons. Or else head protection, hairnets, like the women, so you look branded, like you're being punished. I don't think any of you can imagine how much satisfaction that gave someone like Flemming. Most of them wore head protection and when no one was looking they naturally took it off. With the result that Flemming immediately went through the ceiling. He didn't have anything against long hair, but in the shop . . . *unfortunately* . . . and so on. When I saw the way he'd grin then, I'd just about explode. I don't know what you'd call that when people constantly get harassed because of their hair. I'd like to know who you're hurting with it. I always thought Flemming was a real bastard then. Especially when he said: Look at Edgar. He always looks proper. Proper!

Somebody'd once told me the story about a model student like that, A-average or better, son of splendid parents, only he didn't have any friends. And there was this gang in his neighborhood that tipped over park benches and smashed windows and stuff like that. Nobody could catch them. The leader was an absolutely sly dog. But one more or less beautiful day it happened anyway. They got him. The guy had hair down to his shoulders—typical. Only it was a wig, and the truth was he was that same splendid model student. One day he'd had enough, and he'd gotten himself a wig.

In Berlin at first I thought of getting a wig somewhere, for the "Grosse Melodie." But in the first place wigs don't grow on trees, and secondly, my hair grew at a fantastic rate. Whether you believe it or not—my hair grew approximately two centimeters a day. That had always been a pain in my life. I could hardly get away from the barber. But this way I at least had a respectable mop in two weeks.

"Then you saw him more often after that?"
"That couldn't be avoided. We were after all prac-

tically neighbors. And after the thing with the mural he couldn't get the kids off his back anymore. What else could I have done? He had a way with children, which is something most men don't, I mean, most boys. Besides, I'm convinced that most children know exactly who really likes them and who doesn't."

That's the truth. Charlie's brats couldn't be helped. That's the way kids are. You can't give them an inch. I knew that. They probably think you enjoy it. Just the same, I cooperated, patient as a cow. First of all because Charlie was of the opinion that I got along with children magnificently. Sort of crazy about kids. I didn't want to disillusion her. Me? Crazy about kids? Secondly because the brats were my only chance to stay close to her. Do what I would I couldn't get Charlie back on my kolkhoz, let alone in my garden house. She knew why, and I did too. Day after day I hung around that playground. I pushed the merry-go-round or whatever that thing with the four beams is called, or I played Indian. That way I slowly learned how you can shake them off when you want to. At least for ten minutes. I divided them up into two groups and let them play war.

About that time I got the first answer from Willi. Good Old Willi. That was too much for him. He couldn't get over it. On his tape was the following text: Greetings, Eddie! I don't get it. Give me the new code. Which book, which page, which line? End. What's with variant three?

Give me the new code! That killed me. It was too much for him. It wasn't really fair of me, I admit it. Usually we talked to each other like that—in code. But that was too much. A new code. I could've kicked myself in the ass. When we were in the mood, for example, we'd shoot off dumb proverbs at each other a mile a minute: There are two ends to a loaf of bread.—Right. But when you don't dry the dishes in the morning, they're still wet.—You don't have to be stupid to be dumb.—Work makes your feet dry. In that vein. But *that* was too much for Old Willi. Man, you should have heard his voice. He didn't understand the world anymore. By variant three he meant whether or not I was working. He probably thought I was starving. Just like Charlie. She was always bugging me about it.

I didn't have anything against work. My opinion about it was: when I work, then I work, and when I mess around, I mess around. Or didn't I deserve any vacation? But nobody should think I planned to sit on my kolkhoz forever or something. At first you might think that'll work. But any halfway intelligent person knows how long. Until you go crazy, people. Always to see only your own mug, that just about guarantees you'll go crazy after a while. That just doesn't work anymore. All the fun's gone and everything. For that you've gotta have friends, and a job. At least I do. I just hadn't gotten that far yet. For the time being, it was still OK. Besides, I didn't have any time for work. I had to stick around Charlie. Charlie meant something to me, but I probably already said that. In a case like that you've got to stick around. I can see myself squatting next to her on that playground and the brats were running around us. Charlie was crocheting. An idyll, people. All that was missing was that I didn't have my head in her lap. I didn't have any inhibitions, and I'd already managed it once. The feeling on the back of my head was not bad. Serious. But ever since that day she'd brought her crocheting stuff along and fooled around with it in her lap. She came in the afternoon with her brats, sat down and got out her crocheting stuff. I was always already there. Charlie had a way of sitting down that'd just about make you flip. She probably only had full skirts, and before she sat down she'd grab hold of the hem, lift the whole thing up, and then sit down on her panties. She did that very precisely. That's why I was always right there when she came. I didn't want to miss it. I also always made sure that the bench was dry. I don't know if she noticed, but she knew for sure that I was watching her when she sat down. Nobody can tell

36

me different. That's the way they are. They know for sure that you're watching them, and they do it anyway. It was also a show in itself everytime when she'd look down with her headlights. I think that Charlie had a slight squint. That's why you always got the impression she was looking right at you. I don't know if you've ever seen these portraits of people that hang on the wall and always look at you no matter where you stand. The trick that the painters have is simply that they paint the eyes so the optical axes are exactly parallel, which is never true in real life. It's a known fact that there are no real parallels. By that I don't mean that it wasn't pleasant for me. Not that. It's just that you never knew for sure if she was taking you seriously or making fun of you. That can really bug you.

I probably already said that I'd practically become part of the kindergarten furnishings. A sort of ex-officio caretaker or something. All that was missing was for me to paint the fence. This toy repairing and merry-go-round pushing was just part of the job. And balloon blowing. One day, I think it was a party, I'd already blown up about two to the sixth power balloons and by the two to the seventh power balloon I started to black out, and I fell over. I just fell right over. I could stay under water for four minutes, starve for three days, or go a whole half a day without music, I mean: genuine music. But that made me fall over. When I surfaced again I was lying in Charlie's lap. I noticed that right away. She'd undone my shirt and was massaging my chest. I pressed my skull into her belly and held still. Unfortunately I am insanely ticklish. I had to sit up. The brats were standing around us. Charlie was pale. Almost immediately she burst out: If I was hungry I'd eat!

I protested: It came from all the blowing.

Charlie: If *I* didn't have anything to eat I'd buy myself something.

I grinned. I knew exactly why she was ranting so. Because she was fantastically happy that I was still alive. Any half-way intelligent person could've seen that. She nearly gobbled me up with her headlights, people. I almost went crazy. Only I could've sent the brats to the moon.

Charlie: If *I* didn't have any money, I'd get a job.

I said: He who doesn't eat, shall also not work. I always thought that such distortions were rather clever. Then I got up, shot onto my kolkhoz, which wasn't more than two steps away, and dug up the first head of lettuce that I could get my hands on. I probably haven't told you yet that one day I'd scattered all the seed packages I could find in Willi's garden house in the yard, just as a joke. The first thing to appear was the lettuce. Lettuce and radishes. I started to cram the lettuce down my throat. The sand crunched, but I just wanted to get out the following:

How fortunate it is for me that my heart can feel the plain, naive delight of the man who puts on the table a cabbage that he has grown himself.

Naturally I'd gotten that from that Werther. I guess I had more charm that day than ever.

Charlie just said: You're crazy.

She'd never said that before. She always went right through the ceiling when I came up with this Werther stuff. I wanted to grab my chance and lodge my skull in her lap again, and I guarantee it would've worked, if that stupid Werther paperback hadn't slipped out of my shirt at that moment. I'd gotten into the habit of carrying it in my shirt. I really didn't know why myself.

Charlie got her hands on it immediately. She flipped through it without reading anything. I looked pretty worried. I would've really felt stupid if she'd figured everything out. She asked what it was. I mumbled: toilet paper. A second later I'd grabbed it back again. I put it away. I'd estimate that my hands were shaking the whole time. After that day I left it in the garden house, people. I wanted to keep on playing the charmer and everything, only right then the principal came charging out onto the playground. At first I thought that maybe she had something against my esteemed presence. But she didn't even see me. She only looked at Charlie, sort of strangely.

She said: You can quit for the day. I'll finish up for you.

Charlie didn't understand it at all.

The principal: Dieter is here.

Charlie turned white as a sheet, then bright red. Then she looked at me like I was some kind of criminal, and she took off.

I didn't know what was going on.

The principal explained it to me. Dieter was her fiancé. He'd come home from the army that day, honorable discharge and all. I asked myself how come Charlie didn't know that. They usually write and tell you. Then I thought of the you're-a-criminal look. *I* was the guilty one, *I*, Edgar Wibeau, the lazy kid, the pseudo painter, the crazy man! It was supposed to be my fault that she hadn't met Dieter at the train station with flowers and everything. I felt like I'd been kicked by a horse. I think I already said that I've got a lot of charm. That I was pretty successful with women, with females, I mean. I mean: spiritually, or whatever you want to call it. Sylvia was almost three years older than me, but hardly a woman. I don't know if you can understand me. Sylvia was way below my niveau. I didn't have anything against her for it, but she was way below my niveau. Charlie was the first real woman I'd ever had anything to do with. I hadn't thought that I'd fall for her so fast. I was almost out of my mind, people. I think that happened 'cause I hung around her so much. I shot back into my garden house, that is, I wanted to. But before that I saw Dieter. He was coming toward Charlie. He was wearing a jacket and tie, and he had a suitcase, one of those stupid attaché cases, an air rifle in a case, and a bouquet of flowers. I guessed him to be about twenty-five: I mean, this Dieter. In that case he must have served longer. He'd probably gotten to be a general or something. I waited to see if they'd kiss. But I couldn't see anything.

Back in the garden house I immediately grabbed the mike. Old Willi had to hear about this. About one second and I'd found the appropriate text:

Enough, Wilhelm: the betrothed is here! . . . Fortunate that I was not present to witness his reception! That would have rent my heart. End.

"If his painting wasn't worth anything, I ask myself, how did he actually support himself?"

"At the most he could've gotten a job somewhere as temporary help. But we would have noticed that, my husband and I. That is, we weren't married yet then. We'd known each other for a long time, since we were children. He'd been in the army for a long time. I introduced him to Edgar. Dieter, I mean my husband, had been in charge of garrison duty. I don't know if that means anything to you. Anyway, with that job he came into contact with a lot of boys Edgar's age. I thought that he might have some influence on Edgar. They did get along well together, too. We visited Edgar once, and he was at our place occasionally. But Edgar couldn't be helped. He just couldn't be helped. Dieter really had the patience of Job with him, maybe too much so, I don't know. But Edgar just couldn't be helped."

That's true. They both moved in on me one day. As long as she had Dieter with her Charlie dared to go into my garden house again. She hadn't been on the playground for a few days. Her brats had, but not her. Then she popped up with Dieter at my place. She treated me like a kid. I'd been through that before. She wanted to make it clear to Dieter that she thought of me as a harmless jerk. Immediately I put up my dukes. I mean, not really. On the inside. I probably haven't told you that since I was fourteen I'd been in a boxing club. That and Old Willi were probably the best about

Mittenberg. Of course I didn't know what kind of a partner he was. At first glance I guessed him to be pretty flabby. But I'd learned that you can never judge your partner by first glance. But that he wasn't the right man for Charlie, that was my opinion from the start. He could have been her father, I mean, not according to his age. But otherwise. He carried himself with at least as much dignity as Bismarck or somebody like that. He was looking over my collected works. Charlie'd probably dragged him along mostly for that reason. She still wasn't really sure whether I wasn't really an unrecognized genius. Most of the time she stuck close to Dieter. I still had my dukes up. Dieter was taking a long time. I thought he wasn't going to say anything. But that was the way Dieter was. I don't think he ever said a damn thing in his life that he hadn't thought over three times, or maybe more. Then he began: I would say that it wouldn't hurt him if he were to orient himself more toward real life in the future, toward the life of the construction worker, for example. He has all the subjects he needs practically right outside his door. And then there are naturally here as in all professions certain rules which he simply must observe: perspective, proportion, foreground, background, etc.

That was it. I looked at Charlie. I looked at the man. I could have screamed shit at the top of my lungs. The man meant that all seriously, completely seriously. At first I thought: irony. But he meant that seriously, people.

I could have knocked him around the ring a while longer, but I decided to put my strongest weapon into action. I thought for a moment and then shot out the following gem:

One can say much in favor of rules, about the same things as can be said in favor of civil society. A person who trains himself by the rules will never produce anything absurd or bad, just as one who lets himself be modelled after laws and decorum can never become an intolerable neighbor, never an outright villain; on the other hand any "rule," say what you like, will destroy the true feeling for nature and the true expression of her!

This Werther had really thrown together some worthwhile things. I could see right away that I could safely lower my fists. The man was finished. Charlie had prepared him for at least everything, but *that* was too much for him. He acted as if he were dealing with a maniac who you didn't dare provoke, but he couldn't fool me. Any half-way intelligent trainer would have taken him out of the fight. Technical knockout. Charlie wanted to go then. But Dieter still had something to say: On the other hand it's very original, what he paints, and very decorative.

I don't know what he meant by that. He probably thought *he'd* knocked me out, and now he wanted to sugar-coat the pill. You poor ass! I felt sorry for the man. I let him go. And then, of all stupid things, this silhouette that I'd made of Charlie caught his eye. Charlie said immediately: That's supposed to be for you. He just hasn't given it to me yet. Supposedly because he hasn't finished it yet. But he hasn't *done* anything to it since then.

And Dieter: Now I have you in the flesh.

God! That was probably supposed to be charming. He was a real charmer, dear old Dieter.

Then they split. Charlie'd draped herself around him the whole time. I mean, not really. With her headlights. Just so I saw it. But that ran off me like water off a duck's back. Not that you should think I had something against Dieter because he was in the army. I didn't have anything against the army. I admit I was a pacifist, especially when I thought of the unavoidable eighteen months. Then I was an outstanding pacifist. But I wasn't able to look at any Viet Nam pictures or anything like that. Then I saw red. If somebody'd asked me then, I'd have signed up for the rest of my life. Serious.

I've got one more thing to say about Dieter: He was probably a very nice guy. After all, not everyone could be an idiot like me. And he was probably exactly the right man for Charlie. But there was no point in thinking about it. I can only tell you, people, not to think about it in a situation like that. When you're face to face with your opponent you can't stop to think about whether he's a nice guy or not. That gets you nowhere.

I grabbed the mike and gave Willi the latest:

He wishes me well, and I surmise that that is Lotte's doing . . . , for in that respect women have a fine instinct, and a sound one: if they can keep two admirers on good terms with each other, that is bound to be to their advantage, however rarely it succeeds. End.

I was slowly getting used to this Werther, but I still had to hang in there. I knew that you've got to hang in there, people. You might win the first round, but you can't let up your guard. I stayed hot on their tails and didn't let up. "I'll get you yet," in this vein. Charlie clung to Dieter's arm. She gave her other one amost instantly to me. That almost drove me out of my mind. I had to think of Old Werther. That man knew what was what. Dieter didn't even open his mouth.

We landed in Dieter's apartment. In an old building. One room and a kitchen. That was the tidiest room that I'd ever seen. Mother Wibeau would've loved it. It was about as homey as the waiting room at the train station in Mittenberg. Except that one was at least never straightened up. *That* I could've put up with. I don't know if you know what I mean, these rooms that always look as if they're only lived in two days out of the whole year and then by the head of public health. And the best part was: Charlie suddenly thought the same thing. She said: That's all going to change. Once we're married, right?

I started with a sort of grand tour. First I took a look at the pictures he had. The one was a lousy print of Old Gogh's sunflowers. I didn't have anything against Van Gogh and his sunflowers. But when you start finding a picture hanging in every stupid john it begins to make you sick. At the least it'd make me want to puke. Usually I couldn't stand it for the rest of my life. The other was in one of those convertible frames. I don't want to say anything more about that. Whoever's seen it knows which one I mean. Enough to make you sick, serious. This splendid couple there on the beach. After all: convertible frame. When I want to see all the pictures in the world I'll go to the museum. Or if a picture really gets to me I hang it up in three different places so I can see it no matter where I am. Whenever I saw one of those convertible frames all I ever thought is that the people have committed themselves to look at twelve pictures a year.

Suddenly Charlie said: The pictures go back to our school days.

But I hadn't opened my mouth *once* the whole time. I hadn't even groaned or rolled my eyes or anything. I turned and looked at Dieter. I gotta tell you, the man was standing in his corner, had his fists down, and stood still. Can be that he hadn't yet realized that the second round had already begun. Charlie was constantly making excuses for him, and he didn't budge. People, at least I knew what to do. My next move was to take a look at his books. He had a million of them. All behind glass. All arranged according to their size. I just about flipped. Whenever I saw something like that I just about flipped. I've probably already stated my opinion about books. I don't know what all he had. Guaranteed, all of 'em good books. Marx, Engels, Lenin, all in neat rows. I didn't have anything against Lenin and the others. I also didn't have anything against Communism and all that, the abolition of the exploitation of the world. I wasn't against that. But against everything else. That you arranged books according to their size, for example. It's the same with most of us. They don't have anything against Communism. No half-way intelligent person can have anything against Communism these days. But they're against the other things. Being for something doesn't take courage. But everyone wants to be courageous. Consequently they're against things. That's the way it is. Charlie said: Dieter's going to study German. He's got a lot of catching up to do. Most of them his age who weren't in the army so long have already been assistant professors for a long time now.

I looked at Dieter. If I'd been in his shoes I'd have attacked by now. But he hadn't even put up his dukes yet. A fantastic situation. Slowly I was beginning to see that there was going to be an explosion if I kept this up and if Charlie didn't stop making excuses for him.

The only thing in the whole room was Dieter's air rifle, the kind you can break down. He'd hung it over his bed. I took it down, carelessly, without asking, and started fooling around with it. I aimed it at this couple on the beach, then at Dieter, and then at Charlie. When I got to Charlie Dieter finally leapt into action. He pushed the barrel away.

I asked: Loaded?

And Dieter: Just the same. Too much has happened already.

Grandfather sayings like that one always pissed me off. Still I didn't say anything. I just held the barrel up to my temple and pulled the trigger. That finally brought him out of hibernation: That's not a plaything. Even you've gotta have *that much* sense!

And he grabbed the flintlock away from me.

Then I went for my most powerful weapon, Old Werther:

My friend . . . human beings are human, and the bit of common sense a man may have counts for little or nothing when passions rage and the bounds of humanness press in on us. Say rather—We'll come back to this.

The bounds of humanness, Old Werther wasn't satisfied with any less. But I'd gotten to Dieter. He made the mistake of thinking about what I'd said. Charlie stopped listening altogether. But Dieter made the mistake of thinking about it. I really could've gone. Then Charlie started in: I'll make us something to munch on, OK?

And Dieter: OK with me! But I've got things to do. He

was already in gear. He planted himself behind his desk. With his back to us.

Charlie: He's got to take his entrance exams in three days.

Charlie must've had a bad day. She just wouldn't give up. I was still standing around. That was when Dieter hit the ceiling. He said coldly: You can tell him more about me *along the way*.

Charlie turned pale. We'd just been thrown out, both of us. I'd gotten her into a splendid situation, and I, idiot that I am, was happy about it. Charlie was pale, and I, idiot that I am, stood there and was happy. Then I left. Charlie followed me. When we got out onto the street I managed to get my arm around her shoulder.

Charlie jabbed me in the ribs right away and hissed: Are you crazy?

Then she ran away. She ran away, but I got into a completely crazy mood. Slowly I began to see that it was a losing fight with Charlie. Still and all I was somehow really high. At least I was suddenly standing in front of my garden house with a tape from Old Willi in my paws. Consequently I must have been at the post office. I don't know if you know what I mean, people.

Dear Edgar. I don't know where you are. But if you want to come back now, the key is under the doormat. I won't ask any questions. And from now on you can come home whenever you want. And if you want to finish your apprenticeship in another factory, that's OK too. The main thing is that you are working and not just fooling around.

I thought I'd been kicked by a horse. That was Mother Wibeau.

Then came Willi. Greetings, Eddie! I just *couldn't* get rid of your mother. Sorry. She's really down. She even wanted to give me money for you. Maybe that idea about working isn't so bad. Think about Van Gogh or one of them. All the stuff they had to do just in order to paint. End.

I listened to it, and right away I knew what Old Werther'd have said:

That was a night! Wilhelm! now I can survive anything. I shall not see her again! Here I sit and gasp for air, try to calm myself, and await the morning, and the horses are ordered for sunrise. . .

The stupid tape wasn't any longer, and I didn't have any more in reserve. I could have erased some music, but I didn't want to. To go out and get a new tape would've been a pain too. I analyzed myself quickly and figured out that the whole kolkhoz and everything just didn't turn me on any more. I didn't think of going back to Mittenberg, not that. But it just didn't turn me on any more.

"But sometime or other Edgar must've started working, construction. At WIK."

"Yes, of course. I just lost track of him. I had enough to do. The wedding. Then Dieter started going to the university. German. It wasn't easy for him at first. I was only working half-days, in order to make it easier for him at the start. Then our kindergarten moved into the new building, the old one was torn down, because they were putting up the new ones. The playground next to Edgar's lot went too. We would've only had to go to the police. Somebody's living in the garden house illegally. I don't know if that would've helped him. In any case, then it wouldn't have happened."

"May I ask you something? Did you like Edgar?"

"What do you mean 'like'? Edgar wasn't even eighteen, I was over twenty. I had Dieter. That's all there was to it. What do you think?"

That's right, Charlie. Don't tell everything. There wouldn't be any point to it, telling everything. I've never done it in my whole life. I didn't even tell you everything, Charlie. You can't tell everything. If you tell everything, maybe you're not even human.

"You don't have to answer me."

"Of course I liked him. He could be very funny. Even touching. He was always moving . . . I . . . ."

Stop bawling, Charlie. Do me a favor and stop bawling. I was a loser. I was just some idiot, I was a screwball, just a lot of hot air. Nothing to bawl about. Serious.

"Hi. I'm supposed to speak to a Mr. Berliner."

"Yeah. That's me."

"My name is Wibeau."

"Are you related to Edgar? Edgar Wibeau, the kid who was with us?"

"Yeah. I'm his father."

Addi! You old grubber! How'ya doing? Right from the start you were my best enemy. I pissed you off whenever I could, and you gave me a hard time every way you knew how. But now that it's all over, I can tell you: You're a real stubborn bastard. Our immortal souls were related. Just that your brain waves were straighter than mine.

"That was a tragic thing with Edgar. At first we didn't know what to make of it. Everything's clearer to us now. Edgar was a worthwhile person."

Addi, you disappoint me, and I thought you were a stubborn bastard. I thought you wouldn't go along with all that, saying that bull about somebody who's bitten the dust. Me, a worthwhile person? Schiller and Goethe and those guys, they were maybe worthwhile people. Or Zaremba. It always killed me anyway, when they say that crap about somebody who's dead, what a worthwhile person he was and that. I'd like to know who started it.

"Right from the start we'd misjudged Edgar, that's the truth. We underestimated him, above all me as foreman. From the start all I saw in him was the faker, the good-for-nothing, who wanted to live off the sweat off our backs."

Of course I wanted to earn money. If you want to buy tapes you've got to have money. And where do you get it? Construction! The old saying: If you can't do anything and don't want to, work construction or for the railroad. The railroad was too dangerous for me. I can guarantee they would've asked for my ID and social security number and all that crap. So it was construction. They take everyone. I knew that. I was only ticked 'cause when I came to Addi and Zaremba and the crew they were renovating old Berlin apartments, one right after the other, and Addi said first thing: You say "Good Morning" when you come in here.

I knew *that* type. Ask one of them about Salinger or something. I'll guarantee they won't know. He'd think it was a technical manual that he'd missed.

Could be that everything would've been different if Addi had taken the day off that day or something. But *the way* he acted I felt personally challenged. It could also be that my nerves weren't very good, because of the thing with Charlie. That had gotten to me more than I'd thought.

The next thing Addi did was to hand me one of those paint rollers and ask me if I'd ever had one in my hand before. Every Pioneer* knows those things. Consequently I just refused to answer. After that he handed me a paint brush and sent me over to Zaremba. Undercoat the windows. Everybody's standing around gaping, of course, wondering what I'm going to do. But I felt better as soon as I saw Zaremba. It was sort of love at first sight. Right away I knew that the old guy was a real animal. Zaremba was over seventy. He could've retired a long time ago, but instead he stayed here and worked his ass off. And he wasn't just a stand-in. He could clamp a stepladder between his legs and dance around the room on it without wetting his pants. Be-

---
* Organization for children between the ages of six and thirteen in the German Democratic Republic.

sides the fact that he was only made out of skin, bone, and muscles. Where was the piss supposed to come from, anyway? One of his tricks was to have someone drop an open jackknife on his biceps. It popped back like rubber. Or he'd play the Hunchback of Notre Dame. For that he'd take one of his eyes out—he had a glass eye—bend himself in at the hips and stagger around. He'd gotten a hold of that glass eye in Spain. I mean: It'd been made for him by somebody in Philadelphia. Besides that he was missing part of one of his little fingers and two ribs. To make up for it though he still had all of his teeth and both arms and a chest full of tattoos. But not those fat women and hearts and stuff and anchors. It was filled with flags and stars and hammers and sickels, there was even a part of the Kremlin wall there. He himself was probably from Bohemia or something. But the neatest thing was that he still fooled around with women. I don't know if you're gonna believe me, but it's all true. Zaremba took care of the trailer. He kept it clean and always had the key. It was a pretty nice vehicle. With two bunks and everything to go with it. Once when it was dark I snuck up to it. Until then I didn't know anything, it was just that I had something I had to do under the trailer for a very special reason. I could hear clearly that he was just about to make some woman. Judging by her laughter she must have been very nice. You shouldn't think, however, that I'd have gotten all excited about Zaremba just because of that. No way. Especially not because the first thing he asked me was whether I was paid up on my union dues. He was the treasurer. That really pissed me off. If it hadn't been Zaremba I'd have split right away. Instead I just held out my book. He took it away from me and started snooping through it. Probably he only wanted to know where I stood. Naturally I hadn't paid in Berlin. Right away he got out his goofy little tin box and I was supposed to pay up. That's a real trick, when you can't even afford tapes. He probably just wanted to know that.

Then I started right in putting the undercoat on one of

those windows. The paint ran all over the glass. I'd painted the windows umpteen times at home, but I just couldn't seem to manage it. If they hadn't been gaping so, wondering how I'd react, I'd have whipped off the cleanest window imaginable. Not as clean as Zaremba. Zaremba painted like a machine. But still as clean as any one of them, including Addi. Addi was obviously getting nervous. The only reason he didn't go right through the ceiling was because Zaremba was right next to me. That Zaremba couldn't be bothered was already clear to me. In any case, Addi finally couldn't take it any more and burst out: I was going to smear up the *whole* window.

What I did then is probably obvious. I started to smear up the whole window. I thought Addi was going to fall off his ladder. But then *I* almost fell off my ladder, if I'd been standing on one. Zaremba, who was right next to me, started singing. I thought I'd been kicked by a horse and run over by a bus and both at the same time. Zaremba bellowed away, and right away the others started doing it with him, and it wasn't even a hit or anything, but one of those songs where you only know the first verse. But the crew bellowed out the whole song. I think it was: Arise, you socialists, close the ranks, the drums are calling, the flags now blow . . .*

That was one hell of a crew, people. Arise you socialists! I almost dropped my paintbrush. That was Zaremba's way when Addi was about to go through the ceiling. I found that out the next time it happened. It was in some stupid old kitchen. The wall was pretty cracked and I was supposed to plaster it up. Addi said: Ever worked with plaster before? Then take a look at this wall.

In that vein.

So I started mixing plaster in some old bucket. I don't know if you know about that, people. In any case, all my life I've always put in too much plaster, then too much water,

*From the "Sozialistenmarsch," written by Max Kegel (music by Carl Gramm, 1891).

and so on. At this rate the bucket got slowly full, and I'd have to have been a magician to have kept the stuff from getting hard. I was looking pretty worried. Then help came. Addi blew his cool. He hissed: I'd fill the *whole* bucket.

Nothing better occurred to him. I took him at his word and dumped all the plaster into the bucket. At the exact same time Zaremba started singing. He couldn't even see us from the john or wherever he was hiding. But he must have smelled what was happening. It was another one of his jokes, this time with partisans, and the whole crew joined the fight. He really had them in the palm of his hand. Addi pulled himself together almost instantly and sent me into one of the rooms to sweep the floor for undercoating. If I'd been in his shoes I'd probably have dumped the whole bucket, plaster and all, on my head. But Addi pulled himself together. Then it dawned on me, what this singing was all about. I split. I was just wondering what Zaremba would do if I got to him. If he'd sing. Before that I heard Zaremba storm into the kitchen and snarl at Addi: Take it easy, fellow. Real easy. No?

And Addi: Just tell me, what does he want with us? He just wants to get rich off of our work. No question about it. That no-good.

And Zaremba went: No . . . no-good?!

I probably already said that Zaremba was from Bohemia. That's probably the reason for this "no" business. He managed to get it out at least three times in every sentence. The man could say more with his "no" than other people say in whole novels. If he said "no?" and leaned his head over to the side, that meant: You better think that one over again, fella. If he went: "no?!" and raised his eyebrows at the same time, that meant: Don't say that again, buddy. If he squinted his pig slits everybody knew the Hunchback of Notre Dame was coming. I don't know if that's true. Somebody told me, after '45 Zaremba was supposed to have been the highest judge in Berlin for three weeks or so. He's supposed to have given some really weird and strict sentences.

No? Mr. Defendant, so you were always a good friend of Communism, d'cheer! In that vein. "D'cheer," that was also one of his words. It took me forever to figure out that "d'cheer" meant "did ya hear." Zaremba was a real animal.

I don't know if he got sick of singing or if he finally realized that Addi and I didn't get along. In any case *he* started giving me my orders himself. The first one was that I was supposed to whitewash the panel, I mean the stuff above the panel, in some old bathroom, and the ceiling. He left me alone and I mixed up the prettiest blue goo and started to roll it all over the ceiling and walls, like pop art. After a while it looked like the blueprints for expressway interchanges. And everything in this real neat blue. I wasn't even through, and there was Zaremba, standing there, and the whole crew behind him. They were probably anxious as hell to see what he was going to do with me, especially Addi. But he just went: "No?!"

That was probably the longest "no" I'd ever heard out of him. Besides that he leaned his head over to one side, raised his eyebrows, and squinted his pig slits, all at the same time. I could have burst with pride. I'm still proud of this new "no" variation.

"Sure he acted a little strange. No question about it. But that should've tipped us off, especially me. Instead I chased him away, even Zaremba wasn't able to stop me. Zaremba was maybe the only one of us who'd suspected what Edgar had in him. But I was hardheaded. It has to do with our VPS, vaporless paint sprayer. We'd already built a lot of things, but that was going to be our greatest. A machine that could spray any kind of paint without producing that awful vapor that every other kind of sprayer still makes. That would've been one-of-a-kind, even in the world market. Unfortunately we'd come to a standstill about that time. Not even the experts we called in were able to help. And then Edgar comes along and gives us his two cents worth. I really exploded. I don't want to apologize. I just wasn't all there."

Do me a favor, Addi, and save your breath. I can tell you exactly what I had in me: nothing. And as far as the VPS is concerned: absolutely nothing. Your idea with the air-pressure and the hollow nozzle was lousy, but so was my idea with the hydraulic pressure. So what are you jabbering about? I'll admit that I really thought the hydraulic idea was great, actually from the start, almost as soon as I saw the thing. It was lying around under our trailer. I'd already tripped over it at least three times and had already looked it over. But I'd rather've died than ask someone what kind of machine it was. Especially not Addi. Until one day Zaremba opened his mouth. I think that dog was able to see through me like glass.

Haven't seen it yet, no? Can't, either. It's unique. This paint sprayer sprays every kind of paint under the sun, in the water or in the air, does as much in one day as three painters, no, works *without* this vapor, and for that reason is better than all other comparable machines on the market, even American, d'cheer. That is, when we get it working, no?

Then he wiped a little of the dust off the thing and stood around sighing. And then he said: It's not our first invention, but our best one, no.

It looked as if he wanted to prod the crew on a little, who'd naturally long since been standing there. That thing'd probably been lying around there for a long time. It didn't work at all, it just vaporized and vaporized, and beyond that nothing.

I said: The machine will never replace it.

And I held up my paintbrush. And started undercoating again.

That set off Addi: Listen here, my friend. That's all well and good. I don't know what's eating you, but something is. No question about it. And I don't care. But we're a crew here, and not a bad one, and you belong to it, and in the long run you've got no choice but to fit in and pull your own weight. And don't think you're our first case of that. We've straightened out a lot of others. Ask Jonas. In any case, we're still waiting for the guy who can pull us down to average.

There it was again. He turned around in his tracks and took off, with the others at his heels. I'd only understood about half of what he'd said. The line about the machine was, after all, harmless. I had a lot of other stuff I could've said. From Old Werther, for example. I analyzed the situation quickly and concluded that I'd hit Addi's weakest point with the sprayer.

On top of which Zaremba says: Gotta understand him, no. His baby, the sprayer. Christ, don't mess with it. Either going to be a flop or *the* success, no? His first!

And I:

He is the most punctilious fool that can exist; one step at a time and as fussy as an old woman; a person who is never content with himself, and whom consequently no one else can satisfy.

That was Old Werther again at last. Zaremba opened his pig slits wide and snarled: No! Don't say that!

He was the first one who this Old High German* didn't knock off his horse. That would've made me feel bad. I'll admit I'd picked out a fairly normal passage for him. I don't know if you know what I mean, people. A few days later it came to a showdown. Addi and the crew had set up the

---

* It is customary to divide the history of the German language into three periods. The first of these, Old High German, dates from the beginning of literary tradition about the eighth century to about 1100.

sprayer in the yard of one of these stupid old houses and were hooking it up. Two experts from some specialty shop had come with a whole box full of nozzles, all different. They were all going to be tried out. Big show! Just about everyone and his grandmother had shown up. All the potters and masons and everybody else who hung around in those houses. None of the nozzles worked. Either a stream as thick as your arm came out or it vaporized like a lawn sprinkler. The experts weren't very optimistic from the start, but they still forked over every one of their nozzles. Addi wouldn't give up. He was a stubborn bastard. Until he grabbed for the smallest caliber, and the pressure was too much for it. The old hose exploded, and everybody standing within a radius of ten yards was as yellow as a Chinaman or something. Especially Addi. That drew an incredible laugh from the whole crowd.

The experts said: Forget it. We didn't have any better luck, and we've got everything! Can't be done! Technically unsolvable, at least for the time being. It's not the fault of the nozzles.

And then I came and drew my Werther pistol:

Uniformity marks the human race. Most of them spend the greater part of their time in working for a living, and the scanty freedom that is left to them burdens them so that they seek every means of getting rid of it.

The experts probably thought I was the crew clown. They grinned anyway. But the crew itself came walking slowly up to me, with Addi at the front. They were still wiping the yellow sauce out of their faces. I put up my dukes, just in case, but nothing happened. Addi hissed coldly: Get out of here! Just get out of here, or I won't guarantee anything.

I couldn't see his face really clearly. I still had paint in my eyes. But it sounded as if he was just about to bawl. Addi was over twenty. I don't know when was the last time I bawled. In any case, it was quite a while ago. That was probably why I did, in fact, get out of there. Could be I'd gone a little too far or something. I hope none of you think I'm a chicken, people. As a boxer you're not really allowed to defend yourself anyway. If you hurt somebody you can go to jail. Besides, Zaremba was there, and he was signaling to me: get out of here. Now is the right time. That was, at least for the time being, the end of my guest appearance as a painter at Addi and company.

By the way, the weather that day was rotten. I took off for my kolkhoz. First thing was to dictate a new tape to Old Willi:

And for all this you are to blame who talked me into undergoing this yoke, and prated so much about activity. Activity! . . . I have petitioned the court for my dismissal. . . . Feed this to my mother in a sweet syrup. End.

I thought that fit magnificently.

"I just fired him! Not that we wanted to isolate ourselves. Jonas, for example, is an ex-con. But most of the people that come to us can't do anything and don't want to either. It's not easy to get a crew together that you can begin to do something with."

"You don't have to apologize. Maybe Edgar was only an obstinate faker, rotten-tempered, incapable of fitting in, and lazy, for all I know."

"Take it easy! He was never actually rotten-tempered, at least not around here. And obstinate . . . ? You must have known him better than we did."

"Know him? I haven't seen him since he was five!"

"I didn't know that. I mean, wait a minute. Edgar visited you. He was at your place!"

Shut up, Addi!

"He was raving about it. You have a studio apartment, faces the north, pictures all over the place, perfect disorder."

I said shut up, Addi!

"Excuse me. But I didn't get that from Edgar—I got it from Zaremba."

"When was that supposed to have been?"

"That must've been after we'd fired him, end of October."

"Nobody was at my place."

Unfortunately it's true. I don't know why I went there, but it's true. He lived in one of those magnificently nondescript modern apartments that Berlin's slowly getting full of. I knew his address. But I didn't know it was one of those magnificently nondescript modern apartments. He had an apartment. And it did face the north. I don't know if any of you thinks I'd be stupid enough just to walk up and introduce myself. Hi, Dad, I'm Edgar, in that vein. No way. I was wearing my work clothes. I just said: furnace man, when he opened the door. He wasn't really impressed, but he did believe me. I didn't have any plan, but I was pretty sure it'd work. A pair of blue pants and you're the furnace man. A stupid old jacket and you're the new janitor. A leather bag and you're the man from the telegraph office, etc. People'll believe anything, and you can't even hold it against them. You've just got to know how to do it. Besides, I still had a hammer with me. I took it and banged around for a while on the radiator in the bathroom. He stood in the door and watched me. I needed a little time to get used to him. I don't know if you can understand that, people. To know you've got a father, and then seeing him, they're *not at all* the same thing. He looked about thirty or so. That really surprised me. I had no idea. I always figured he was at least fifty! I don't know why. He was standing in the door in his bathrobe and a pair of brand new jeans. Around that time you were suddenly able to get real jeans in Berlin. No idea why. But you could. It was like always just before something. The rumor spread, at least in certain circles. They were selling them in some warehouse, because they knew that no department store in Berlin was big enough for people who'd come for those jeans. And there were millions of 'em. I guess none of you'll think that I wouldn't have been there. And how! I hadn't gotten up so early in years, just to be there on time. I'd have kicked myself in the ass if I hadn't gotten any jeans. There were about three thousand of us standing there in this hallway waiting to get in. You can't imagine how crowded it was. That was the day of the first snow, but I can guarantee that none of us froze to death. A couple of people had music with them. It was an atmosphere like at Christmas, when you get up in the morning and start opening gifts—that is, if you still believe in Santa Claus. We were all on a genuine high. I was just about ready to do my Bluejeans Song, when they opened up the door and the show began. Standing behind the doors were four full-grown salesmen. We just pushed them out of the way and plunged into the jeans. Unfortunately the whole thing was a waste. They weren't genuine, the ones they had. They were authentic, but not genuine. Just the same, it was a real happening that day. The funniest thing was probably these two old mummies from the boonies who were standing there in the hallway. They probably wanted to get some genuine jeans for their little boys back in Podunk. But when the mood reached its high point they got weak knees. They wanted out, the dears. They wouldn't have had a chance, even if one of us had helped them. They had to stay, like it or not. I just hope they at least halfway survived.

In any case, this father of mine must have been somewhere in the crowd that day. I was easily able to imagine it while he was standing there in the doorway watching over me. Why he was standing there, that was clear to me right away. There was a pair of women's stockings hanging from a clothesline in the bathroom. I'd have guaranteed he had one in his room, and *that's* where I wanted to look before I gave myself away. So I said: Everything's OK here. Wanta take a look in the other room.

And he: Everything there is OK.

I: Fine. But this is the last time we're coming this year.

Then he gave in. We went into the other room. The woman was lying in bed. Next to the bed was one of those camping cots, that he'd probably camped in. I liked the woman right away. She had something of Charlie. I'm not sure what. Probably it was her way of always looking at you, of always aiming her headlights right at you. Right away I started imagining the three of us living there together. We'd have gotten a hold of a wider bed, or I'd have slept on the old one, or for that matter, on the camping bed in the hallway. I'd have gone and gotten rolls in the morning and made coffee, and we'd have all three of us eaten breakfast together in their bed. And at night I'd have dragged them both to the "Grosse Melodie" or sometimes her alone, and we'd have flirted with each other, decently, of course, like buddies.

Then I turned on my charm: Pardon me, Madam. Only the furnace man. Be done in a sec. In that vein.

I went for the radiator. I tapped on the pipes with the hammer and listened for the echo, like those furnace guys always do. Naturally I was looking over the whole room at the same time. Wasn't much there. Portable shelves with books. A TV, last year's model. Not a single picture in the whole place. The woman offered me a smoke.

I said: No thanks. Smoking is one of the main obstacles to communication.

I was playing the role of the young, well-trained specialist. Then I asked this father of mine: You're not much of a picture fan, are you?

He didn't get it.

I went on: I mean the walls. Tabula rasa. We get around. Everybody's got pictures, always different kinds, but you? But then, you've got other nice things.

The woman smiled. She'd gotten it instantly. But then, it probably wasn't all that difficult. We looked at each other for a second. I think she was the only thing in the whole room that didn't bug me. Everything else bugged me, especially the bare walls. That's the only way I can explain the fact that I suddenly started to babble like a fool: But that makes good sense. I always say, if you're gonna have pictures, then at least ones you've painted yourself, and naturally you don't hang those on your own walls if you've got any sense at all. Do you mind my asking: Do you have any children? Take a tip from me: Kids can paint so it'll just knock you over. You can hang 'em on the wall any time without being embarrassed. . . .

I don't know what other stupid things I might have said. I don't think I stopped talking until I was standing on the stairs, the door was already shut, and it suddenly occurred to me that I hadn't said a word about who I was and all that. But I just couldn't bring myself to ring the doorbell again and say it all. I don't know if you can understand that, people.

When it was all over I crawled back into my garden house, like always. I wanted to hear some music, and I did, too, but somehow it just didn't do anything for me. By then I knew myself well enough to know that something was wrong with me. I analyzed myself quickly and concluded that I wanted to start building *my own* sprayer, right away. *My* VPS. Of course I didn't know how. I only knew it would have to be completely different from Addi's. And I did know that it wasn't going to be easy without the right tools and all that. But it was never like me to let stuff like that scare me off. It was also clear the whole thing had to take place in secret. And then, when it worked, my sprayer, I'd show up at work with it, real casual like. I don't know if you know what I mean, people. In any case, I, idiot that I am, started combing the whole damn deserted subdivision for usable objects that same day. I don't know if you can imagine what

61

all you can find in a place like that. I can only tell you, everything, serious, except what I needed. Just the same I dragged it all home, everything that looked halfway useful. First collect your material, I thought. That was the first stone on my grave, people, the first nail in my coffin.

"I could say that we got him back here pretty quickly again. But that was more on Zaremba's initiative than anybody else's. In principle it was already too late. Edgar'd already started working on *his* VPS. Zaremba didn't know that. We hunted him up in his garden house. But there was no trace of the fact that he was working on it. And we never thought of looking in the kitchen."

That with the kitchen wouldn't have done you a damn bit of good. It was locked up. I wouldn't have let anybody in there. Maybe not even Charlie. I was building away like mad. Then I saw Zaremba's skull with his moldy hair pop up from behind the hedge. Instantly I closed up shop. I threw myself on the stupid old sofa and started coughing. Not that I was sick or anything, at least not really. I did have a cough. Probably I'd gotten it rummaging around in the old subdivision. Maybe I should've already started heating the place. But I could've stopped coughing if I'd wanted to. Only that I'd sort of gotten used to it. It had such a splendid effect. Edgar Wibeau, the unrecognized genius, selflessly works on his newest invention, his lung half eaten away, and he doesn't give up. I was a complete idiot, I mean really. But that spurred me on. I don't know if you understand me. So I was hacking away when the crew stormed into my kolkhoz. I mean, they didn't really storm into it. They came in quietly. First Addi and then Zaremba. Probably the old man was shoving him. These guys obviously thought they were supposed to have a bad conscience or something. 'Cause they'd chased me away. And then me with my cough on the sofa! I don't know if you can imagine what a splendid cough I'd developed. Besides that, my feet were sticking out from underneath this stupid old blanket, as if it was too short.

For Zaremba it was too much! Ahoy! You've never coughed better in your life, no? And then he stepped aside, so that Addi could get out his speech. At first Addi was looking for something to hold onto, then he started in: What I wanted to tell you, sometimes I'm maybe a little too quick to react, that's just my way, no doubt about it. Both of us oughta think about that in the future. And it's all over now with the sprayer. All over and done with, no doubt about it.

It wasn't easy for him. I was almost touched. I couldn't say anything, because of the cough. Jonas, the reformed ex-con, took care of the rest: We thought you could specialize in floor covering. Roller 1 a would be OK too. And on Saturdays we always go bowling.

Naturally the rest of the crew had gathered around in the meantime, in full strength. They'd just trickled in on me, one by one. I had the feeling that Addi or Zaremba had set up guards on all four sides, just in case I'd tried to disappear. I could've laughed my ass off. They were all standing around gaping at my collected works. It was obvious they thought they were dynamite. They thought I was a rare bird, someone you didn't dare get too close to. Except for Zaremba. I'd guarantee Zaremba had his thoughts about me. He started sniffing around my castle. At last he started to open the door to the kitchen. But it was locked, like I said, and as for all his trick questions, like whether or not I was going to stay here all winter, I could hardly answer them. This cough was really unpredictable. It came at the dumbest times, people. I really had a good one. Zaremba wanted to rush me to a doctor, the dog. For a second I must've looked pretty worried. Then it occurred to me that I get this cough every fall and that it's completely harmless. An allergy. Hay fever or something. One of a kind. A riddle for science. And then it'd suddenly stop. But my cough improved amazingly after that day, that is: it vanished, except for occasional minor attacks.

A doctor, that's all I would've needed. My opinion about doctors is: I can live without 'em. I went to a doctor once, because of a rash on my feet. Half an hour later I was on this table, and he was jabbing two shots into every one of my toes. And then he pulled out my toe-nails. That was already outrageous. And when he finished, he sent me off to the waiting room, on foot, people, believe it or not. I was bleeding through the bandages like a wildman. He didn't even think about putting me in a wheelchair or giving me anything. Since then I haven't changed my opinion about doctors.

In any case, from that day on I was on the list of endangered species, as far as Addi was concerned. All those pictures and on top of that an unsurpassed cough. I probably could've afforded to do even more after that. But I was able to control myself. I had no real yearning to host them again on my kolkhoz. They could've caught on to the sprayer. I, idiot that I am, thought the whole time that I'd make headlines with my sprayer. I denied myself almost everything. I didn't even draw my Werther pistol once, for example. I painted my floors with the roller like a good little boy, and Saturdays I sometimes even went bowling. I sat there with ants in my pants, while they bowled and thought to themselves: This Wibeau, we've done a splendid job of straightening him out. It was as bad as in Mittenberg. And at home my sprayer was waiting.

About this time I managed to scare up that Huguenot Museum, by accident. I'd actually long since given up looking for it. At first I'd asked dozens of people, a sort of public opinion poll. Can you tell me where I can find the Huguenot Museum? With zero success. Not one damn person in all of Berlin knew anything about it. Most of them thought I was stupid, or maybe a tourist. And suddenly I was standing right there before it. It was in a dilapidated church. The building had interested me, because it was the first war ruin I'd ever seen. Not one shot had been fired in Mittenberg!

General Brussilow or somebody had forgotten to capture it. And on the only entrance to the whole building that was still intact was: Huguenot Museum. And under that: closed for renovation. Normally I wouldn't have paid any attention to a sign like that. I was after all a Huguenot, and they couldn't shut me out. According to my estimates the head of the place would probably slobber all over me. A genuine, living descendant of the Huguenots. And far as I knew, we were in danger of dying out. But for some reason I stopped dead in my tracks in front of this sign. I analyzed myself quickly and concluded that I wasn't even interested in knowing whether or not I was noble, or what the other Huguenots were up to; probably not even whether I was a Huguenot or a Mormon or something else. For some reason I wasn't even interested any more.

On the other hand it was about this time that I got another crazy idea, namely writing to Charlie.

Since that one day I practically hadn't even seen her. It was clear to me that she'd made up with her Dieter a long time ago and that after all that had happened I didn't have a chance any more. I still couldn't get her out of my mind. I don't know if you know what I mean, people. My first thought was right away Old Werther. He'd written letters to his Charlotte nonstop. It didn't take long for me to find an appropriate one:

If you saw me, best of women, in this surge of distractions! and saw how desiccated my senses become; . . . not one hour of bliss! nothing! nothing!

I scribbled that on the back of a menu in this bowling alley. But I never sent it. It became clear to me, that I just didn't have a chance with her any more with Werther. That wouldn't work with her any more. It was just that I couldn't think of anything else. Just to go there wouldn't work. And then one night there was an envelope in my mailbox. I saw it already from a distance. I'd always had to pick up my mail at the post office. And there wasn't any stamp on it. In it was a card from Charlie: Are you still alive? Drop in some time. We've been married for ages.

Charlie must have been there herself. I almost fell out of my tree, people. My knees were knocking. Serious. I got the shivers. I left everything where it was and tore out of there, but fast. Eight minutes later I was standing in front of Dieter's door. I just assumed they'd be living together at Dieter's. And they were, too. Charlie opened the door. At first she just stared at me. I had the feeling that I hadn't exactly arrived at the right time. I mean, it was the right time, but not *exactly* the right time. Maybe she thought I wouldn't come the same day she'd brought the letter to my kolkhoz. In any case, she asked me in. They only had this one room. Dieter was sitting there. He was sitting behind his desk, exactly like he'd been sitting there a few weeks ago. That is, he wasn't sitting behind it, but rather in front of it. He'd put the desk in front of the window, and was sitting in front of it, with his back to the room. I understood that completely. If you've only got one room, and you've got to work in it too, you've got to be able to block yourself off somehow. And Dieter did it with his back. His back was practically a wall.

Charlie said: Turn around!

Dieter turned around, and fortunately I got an idea: Only wanted to ask if you had a pipe wrench.

I just couldn't get rid of the feeling that Dieter wasn't supposed to know that Charlie'd invited me. I went at the most one step into the room. Oddly enough Charlie said: Do we have a pipe wrench?

I analyzed the situation instantly and came to the conclusion that Charlie was only playing along with the thing with the pipe wrench. Right away I got the shivers again. Dieter asked: What do you need a pipe wrench for? Pipe burst?

And I: You could call it that.

By the way, I really did need this pipe wrench. For the sprayer. I'd scared up something like it in an old shed. Just that it was so dilapidated that the most you could've done with it would've been to chop a hole in your knee. Then we gave each other five, and Dieter went: Well?

That was his uncle-type well. All that was missing was if he'd added: Young man. Have we mended our ways since our last meeting, or do we still have those foolish ideas in our heads? Usually that drove me right up a tree, and this time too. I was up there in a matter of seconds. But I pulled myself together and came down again and played the humble, reasonable, mature young man, that I after all had just become, people. I don't know if you can imagine that, me being humble. And all that just because I thought I had this sprayer in my back pocket, idiot that I am. I don't even know anymore what I was actually thinking. I was probably just so certain that my idea with the hydraulics was exactly right that I was already beginning to act humble like a great inventor after his success. Edgar Wibeau, the great, congenial young man, who has nevertheless remained humble and so on. Like with these top-flight athletes. Man, people, was I ever an idiot. Besides I could naturally see that Charlie was turning red. I mean, I didn't *see* it. I just couldn't look at her the whole time. Otherwise I probably would've done something really stupid. But I *noticed* it. She probably thought that one of her greatest dreams was being realized, that Dieter and I were becoming good friends. Until then she'd been standing behind me in the door. Then she got all excited, wanted to make tea and all that, and I was supposed to sit down. The room was hardly recognizable. It wasn't just that it'd been renovated and all, but it had been completely refurnished. I don't mean with furniture. Actually only the pictures and the lamps and curtains, and all sorts of knick-knacks that Charlie'd probably brought into the marriage with her, were new. Suddenly I wanted to live there myself.

I don't mean that everything was perfectly matched. The chairs with the carpet. The carpet with the curtains. The curtains with the wallpaper and the wallpaper with the chairs. That sort of thing always bugged me. That's not what I mean. But the pictures, for example, were from the brats in the kindergarten. That kids can paint so that it just about knocks you over, I've probably already said that. One of the pictures was probably supposed to be a snowman. He was only with red crayon. He looked like Charlie Chaplin, after he'd been robbed of everything. He could really get to you. Next to it was Dieter's air rifle. All the books suddenly looked as if someone was always reading them. You suddenly felt the urge to plop yourself down somewhere and read every one of them. I started running back and forth in the room, looking at everything and talking about it. I praised everything like a fool. I can only tell you, if you're hot for a woman or a girl, you've got to praise her. In my case that was just a part of the standard service. Naturally I wasn't clumsy about it. More like I was doing, for example, right now in this room with Charlie. Entirely aside from the fact that I *really did* like it, I naturally saw that Charlie was turning alternately red and white. I considered it possible that Dieter'd never said a thing about all that. Which was entirely consistent with the fact that he immediately started to block himself off again. He was working again. When Charlie saw that, she sat down immediately and I had to too. I almost flipped. She always had this way of setting herself down with her skirt. People, I can't even describe what that did to me. Later she motioned me out of the room. Outside she explained to me: You've got to understand him, OK? He's *completely* out of everything because of all that time in the army. He's the oldest in his class. I suspect he doesn't even know for sure if literature is the right thing for him. She was just about whispering. Then she asked me: And you? how's your garden house?

I automatically started in coughing. Decently, of course.

Right away Charlie: You're not going to try to spend the winter there?

I said: Hardly.

Now I was coughing like never before.

Then she asked me: Are you working?

And I: 'Course. Construction.

You could see right away that that turned her on. Charlie was one of those people who you could ask if they believed in the "good in mankind" and they could answer "yes" without turning red. And she was probably thinking that the good in me had finally won out and maybe because she'd been so frank with me that time before.

Whenever I read in some book that somebody was suddenly standing somewhere and didn't know how he'd gotten there, 'cause he was so deep in thought, I usually just bailed right out. I always thought that was a complete crock. But that night I was standing in front of my garden house and really didn't know how I'd gotten there. I must have been sleeping the whole way home or something. I immediately turned the recorder on. First I wanted to dance half the night, but then I started working on my sprayer like a madman. That night I was more certain than ever that I was on the right path with my sprayer. I was only sorry that I hadn't really taken Charlie's pipe wrench with me. Naturally that wasn't even brought up again. Mine was just plain rotten. But this way at least I had a good reason for turning up at Charlie's the next day. Dieter wasn't home. Charlie was tinkering away on the shade of one of her ceiling lamps. It wasn't holding. She was standing on a stepladder, like the ones we used on the job. One of those like Zaremba could dance on. I climbed up next to her, and we worked away together on the dumb lampshade. Charlie held it and I screwed. Believe it or not, people, my hand was shaking. I just couldn't get a grip on this grub screw. After all I'd never actually had Charlie so close to me as then. I probably still could've managed it. But she was aiming her headlights directly at me. It got to the point where I held and Charlie screwed. At any rate that was the best thing for the screw. She finally got it. Our arms were about ready to fall off. I

69

don't know if you know what that's like, when you hold your arms up in the air for hours at a time. If you've ever painted ceilings or put up curtains you know what I mean. We were groaning in unison and massaging our arms, all that on the ladder. Then I started telling her about Zaremba, and how he could dance with the ladder, and then we held onto each other and wobbled around the room on the ladder. We almost tipped over about three times, but we'd made up our minds to get all the way to the door without getting down, and we finally made it. I talked her into it. That was just it: You could talk Charlie into something like that. Ninety-nine out of a hundred women would've given up or else they'd have shrieked a few times and then jumped down. Not Charlie. When we got to the door, Dieter was standing there on the threshold. Right away we jumped down off the ladder. Charlie asked him: Do you want to eat?

And I: I'll go then. I only came for the pipe wrench.

I was scared to death that he was going to grab a hold of Charlie right there in front of me and maybe kiss her or something. I don't know what would've happened then, people. But Dieter didn't even think of it. He went straight to his desk with his briefcase. Either he never kissed Charlie when he came home, or he restrained himself because of me. Right away I had to think of Old Werther, how he writes to his friend Wilhelm:

Yes, and he is so decent that he has not kissed Lotte a single time in my presence. God reward him!

To tell the truth I didn't understand what that had to do with decency, but I understood everything else. In my whole life I never thought that I'd understand this Werther so well. Beyond that, though, he couldn't have kissed Charlie anyway. She took off for the kitchen pretty fast. Still I really should have gone. But I stayed. I put the ladder away. Then I stood around in the room. I wanted to start a conversation with Dieter, only I couldn't think of anything. Suddenly I had the air rifle in my mitts. Dieter didn't utter a word. When

Charlie came back with the snack, she blurted out: Got an idea, men, OK? We'll all go shooting together, by the railroad embankment. You always wanted to teach me how.

Dieter snarled: Light's not good enough this late.

He was against it. He wanted to work. He thought that was kids' stuff. Just like with the ladder. But Charlie aimed her headlights directly at him, and he gave in.

The bad part about it for him was that he just didn't take part at the railroad embankment. We shot at an old parking sign that I pretty quickly ripped to shreds. That is: Charlie shot. Dieter gave the fire orders, and I corrected Charlie's technique. That just happened that way, 'cause it never crossed Dieter's mind to pay attention to Charlie. He just let the children play, so to speak. He was probably thinking of all the time this was costing him. I could see his side, but I still felt like knocking myself out for Charlie. I showed her how to pull the butt into your shoulder and how to stand with your feet at right angles to each other and that you start high and come down into the target and exhale while you're doing it, and I told her all that stuff from my pre-military training that they teach you there. Full sight, fine sight, medium sight, trigger slack and all that. Charlie shot and shot and willingly let me take hold of her until she noticed what was happening with Dieter or maybe until she finally *wanted* to take notice. Then she stopped. Dieter, by the way, had been right, it actually was too dark. Only Dieter had to promise to take her someplace the next Sunday, anywhere, the main thing was to get out. I wasn't mentioned, at least not explicitly. Charlie was really clever about that. She said: . . . let's go someplace.

That must've included me. But maybe I, idiot that I am, just imagined it. Maybe she really wasn't thinking about me. Maybe everything that happened wouldn't have happened if I, idiot that I am, hadn't flattered myself into thinking Charlie'd invited me. But I don't regret anything. Not one damn bit.

Next Sunday I was sitting next to Charlie on their couch in their room. It was raining like crazy. Dieter was sitting at his desk working, and we were waiting for him to finish. Charlie was already in her raincoat and everything. She hadn't even acted surprised or anything when I rang. Everything seemed to go perfectly. Or maybe she was surprised and just didn't show it. This time Dieter was *writing*. With two fingers. On the typewriter. He was writing right out of his head. A paper, I thought, and that was probably right. I could tell right away. It just wasn't flowing. I know what that's like. He was typing about one letter per half hour. That just about says it all. Finally Charlie said: You can't *force* it!

Dieter didn't respond. I had to look at his legs the whole time. He'd wound them around the chairlegs and hooked himself in with his feet. I didn't know if that was a habit of his. But it was obvious to me from the start that he wasn't coming with us.

Charlie started in again: Come on! Just leave everything where it is, OK? That can do wonders!

She wasn't furious or anything. Not yet. She was maybe about as gentle as a nurse is supposed to be.

Dieter said: Not with a boat in this weather.

I don't know if I already told you, but Charlie wanted to rent a boat.

Charlie shoots back: OK. Not a boat, a steamboat. Dieter was actually right. A boat in this weather was crazy.

He started typing again.

Charlie: OK. Not a steamboat. Just a couple of times around the block.

That was her last offer, and it really was a chance for Dieter. But he wouldn't budge.

Charlie: After all, we're not made out of sugar.

I think it was then that she lost her patience. Dieter answered calmly: Go then.

And Charlie: But you promised.

Dieter: I just said: Go!

Then Charlie got loud: We're going!

Just then I left. Anybody would've been able to figure out what was going to happen next. I was really out of place. I mean: I left the room. I really should've gone altogether. I realize that. But I just couldn't bring myself to do that. I stood around in the kitchen for a while. I was suddenly reminded of Old Werther, where he says:

Satiety and indifference, that is what it is! Does not any miserable business matter attract him more than his precious, delicious wife?

Dieter wasn't, of course, a business man, and Charlie was anything but the precious and delicious wife. And it wasn't a matter of satiety with Dieter either. Sure, Dieter must've gotten a pretty big scholarship because of the army. But I'd guarantee that guys like me got at least three times as much just daubing a little paint. I didn't know what it was. Personally I didn't have anything against Dieter, but it was a fact that it'd been an eternity since he'd taken Charlie out. That was the only thing that was a fact. About the same time I'd finished analyzing that, Charlie came shooting out of their room. I'm saying that purposely, people: shooting. All she said to me was: Let's go!

I was right with her.

Then she said: Wait!

I waited. She grabbed this gray poncho from a hook and shoved it into my chest. Dieter'd probably brought it back from the army. It smelled like rubber, gasoline, cheese, and burnt garbage.

She asked me: Can you drive a motorboat?

I said: Hardly.

Normally I'd have said: 'Course. Only I'd done such a good job of taking on the role of the well-behaved young man that I just went ahead and told the truth.

Charlie asked: What'd you say?

She looked at me as if she hadn't heard me right.

Right away I said: 'Course.

Three seconds later we were on the water. That is, it must have taken an hour or so. It's just that for the second time now being with Charlie gave me the feeling as if I didn't know how I'd gotten where I was. Like in a movie. Zoom—and you're there. Only I didn't have any time then to analyze it. This stupid boat had a lot of horsepower. It shot over the Spree like crazy, and on the other side was a concrete wall from some factory. I had a lot of trouble making the curve. Instead of just letting up on the gas, idiot that I am. We'd have drowned for sure, and there'd have been nothing left of the boat. These boats take right off when you start them. No transmission or anything. I looked at Charlie. She didn't make a sound. I guess the boat guy we got the thing from just about flipped. I saw him just standing there on the dock. How Charlie was ever able to weasel that boat out of him, that's a story in itself. I don't know if you'll believe me, that I was really shy and all. Or that I had inhibitions. But I'd have passed when I saw that shed for the FGY* boat rental. Everything was dripping wet. Not a single boat in the water. You couldn't, after all, have called it the "season" anymore, so close to Christmas. And the shed was boarded up like for World War III. But Charlie found a hole in the fence and rang the boat guy out of the shed and pleaded so long with him that he finally handed over the boat from his boathouse. I wouldn't have thought it'd be possible. The boat guy probably wouldn't either. I think Charlie could've gotten *anything* that day. She just couldn't have been held back. She could've talked anybody into anything.

Out on the water she crept in under the poncho with me. It was still raining like crazy. Couple of degrees lower and we'd have had the most beautiful snowstorm ever. Probably none of you still remember last December. It was really cold as hell in the boat, but I didn't even notice. I don't

* Free German Youth ("Freie Deutsche Jugend").

know if you know what I mean. Charlie laid her arm over my seat and her head on my shoulder. I just about flipped. I was slowly getting a feel for the boat. I didn't know if there were traffic laws for on the water. Seemed like I'd heard something about that. But that day there wasn't a single boat or steamer out on the whole damn Spree. I opened it up. The bow shot up in the air. This boat wasn't bad. It was probably for this boat guy's private use. I started making all sorts of curves. Mostly to the left, because that pressed Charlie up against me. She didn't have anything against it. Later she started steering herself. Once we just missed a pier. Charlie didn't say a word. She still had just about the same look on her face as when she'd come shooting out of their room.

Until then I hadn't known that you can see a city from behind. Berlin from the Spree, that's Berlin from behind. All the old factories and warehouses.

At first I thought the rain was going to fill the boat. But it didn't. Probably we drove right out from underneath it. We were already soaked to the bone, in spite of the poncho. There was nothing you could've done about the rain anyway. We were so wet that we didn't even care anymore. We might as well have gone swimming with our clothes on. I don't know if you know what I mean, people. You're so wet you just don't even care.

Somewhere or other the warehouses stopped. Only villas and stuff. Then we had to turn, either left or right. Naturally I picked left. I was only hoping we'd get out of this lake again. I mean: a different way. My whole life I've never liked taking the same way back that I'd come. Not because I'm superstitious or anything. Not that. I just didn't like to. Probably it bored me. I think that was one of my ticks. Like with the sprayer, for example. As we thundered past an island Charlie looked uneasy. She had to go. I got the message. That always happens when it rains. I looked for a gap in the reeds. Fortunately there were a lot of them. Actually more gaps than reeds. It was still coming down in buckets. We jumped onto the shore. Charlie disappeared some-where. When she got back we crouched together in this sopping wet grass on the island. Could be it was only a peninsula. I never went back there. Then Charlie asked me: Want a kiss?

People, I just about flipped. I started shaking. Charlie was still pissed at Dieter, that was obvious. Still I kissed her. Her face smelled like laundry that was bleached about twenty times. Her mouth was ice cold, probably from all that rain. I just couldn't let go of her. She opened her eyes wide, but I just couldn't let go of her. She was really soaked to the bone, her legs and everything.

In some book I once read how this Negro, I mean this Black, comes to Europe and gets his first white woman. He started singing, some song from his homeland. I bailed right out. That was maybe one of my biggest mistakes, always to bail out when I didn't know something. With Charlie I really could've started singing. I don't know if you know what I mean, people. There was no saving me.

Then we went back to Berlin, the same way we'd come. Charlie didn't say anything, but suddenly she was in a big hurry. I didn't know why. I thought that it was just too cold for her. I wanted to get her under the poncho again, but she wouldn't, and she wouldn't say why. She wouldn't even touch the poncho when I gave her the whole thing. The whole way back she didn't say anything. I started feeling like a criminal. I started making curves. Right away I could see she was against it. She was just in a hurry. Then we ran out of gas. We paddled up to the next bridge. I wanted to go to the next station and get gas while Charlie waited. But she got out. I couldn't stop her. She got out, ran up this dripping wet iron stairway, and was gone. I don't know why I didn't run after her. When I'd been at the movies and had seen those films where the woman is always wanting to leave and he wants to stop her, and she runs out the door, and he just stands in the doorway and yells after her, I'd always bailed out. Three steps and he could've had her. And I still just sat there and let Charlie go. Two days later I had bitten the dust, and I, idiot that I am, just sat there and let her go, and just thought about how I was going to get the boat back by myself. I don't know if any of you ever thought about dying and that. About the fact that one day you're just not there any more, no longer present, over and done with, gone, passed away, and irreversibly so. For a long time I thought about that a lot, but then I gave up. I just wasn't able to imagine what that would be like, in the coffin, for example. I could only think of stupid things. Like that I'd be lying in the coffin, and it'd be completely dark, and then I'd get this awful itch on my back, and I'd have to scratch myself or I'd die. But it'd be so narrow that I couldn't move my arms. That's almost half dead, people, if you know what I mean. But I was only, at the most, in suspended animation. I just couldn't do it. Could be, if you can, you're already half dead, and I, idiot that I am, probably thought I'd live forever. I can only advise you, people, never to just sit there and think about a shitty boat or something while someone you really care about's running away.

In any case, this boat guy had as much as alarmed the port authority by the time I finally got back with the boat. He was so happy to have gotten his boat back he could've shit. I thought: He won't forget this day either. At first I thought he was going to make a scene. I put up my dukes. I was in just the right mood. The guy at the service station, for example, I'd given him so much shit he almost fell over. He didn't want to give me a gas can. He was one of those types: Who's-going-to-pay-for-the-can-when-you-don't-come-back-with-it? I can't live with people like that.

At home I hung up my wet things on a nail. I didn't know what to do. I *just didn't* know what to do. I was down like never before. I played the MS. I danced till I was all worked up, maybe about two hours, but I still didn't know what to do. I tried sleeping. But I tossed and turned for 3 hours and a day on the dumb old sofa. When I woke up W. W. III had broken out. A tank attack or something. I jumped up from the dumb old sofa and ran to the door. There was an animal with caterpillar tracks and an iron shield headed right for me. A bulldozer. Hundred-fifty HP. I'd estimate I started bellowing like an idiot. He stopped about a half a yard in front of me, and throttled his engine down. This guy, the driver, came down from his seat. Without any warning or anything he hit me with his right, so that I flew about two yards back into my garden house. I did a backwards somersault. That's the best way to get back on your feet again. I pulled in my head for a counterattack.

I'd have given him a left hook that would have knocked him out. I don't think I've told you yet that I'm left-handed. That was about the only thing that Mother Wibeau couldn't break me of. She tried just about everything she could think of, and I, idiot that I am, went right along with it. Until I started stuttering and wetting the bed. That's when the doctors said stop. I was allowed to write with my left hand again, and I stopped stuttering and slept dry. The result was that later I made out fabulously with my right, better than most people with their left. But the left was still always a little better. Only that this tank driver didn't think of putting up his fists. He suddenly turned snow white and sat down on the ground. Then he said: A second later and you'd a been mush and I'd a been in the can. And I've got three kids. Are you crazy, still living here?

He was clearing the ground with his scraper for the new buildings. I probably looked pretty worried. I mumbled: Just a couple of days and I'll be gone.

One thing became clear to me in the course of that night, that there was nothing left for me in Berlin. Without Charlie there was nothing left for me. That's what it

78

amounted to. Of course *she'd* started the whole kissing business. But slowly I began to see that I'd still gone too far. As the man I should've kept things under control.

Then he said: Just three days. Till after Christmas. Then you're out. Got it?!

Then he swung himself back into his tank. I was determined to finish the sprayer as fast as possible, but three days, that was tight. And I didn't want to miss work. I didn't want to take any risks at the last minute by missing work. Zaremba would've popped up within twenty-four hours and sniffed out the truth. Or Addi. I was, after all, his greatest pedagogic success. I wanted to finish the sprayer, slam it down on the table in front of Addi and then take off for Mittenberg and as far as I was concerned even finish my apprenticeship. I'd come that far. I don't know if you understand me, people. Probably I was just getting soft 'cause of Christmas. I'd actually never put a whole lot of stock in this Christmas stuff. "Hark! what mean those holy voices" and Christmas trees and cookies. But I'd still gotten soft somehow. That's probably why I went *straight* to the post office to see if there was another tape there for me from Willi. Otherwise I'd always waited until after work.

I got a funny feeling when I found a special delivery letter from Willi in my box. I tore it open. I almost flipped. The most important sentence was . . . say what you want to. I couldn't hold out any longer. I told your mother where you are. Just so you won't be surprised when she shows up. He'd mailed it two days before. I knew what I had to do. I took off, instantly. If she took the early train from Mittenberg, she'd have already had to be there, even allowing for stopovers. That meant I still had a chance, till the evening train. I bought an armful of milk cartons, because milk fills you up fastest, and locked myself in my garden house. I closed all the curtains. Beforehand I put a note on the door: Be right back!

79

Just in case. That'll also work for the next stupid bull-dozer. I thought. Then I hurled myself at my sprayer. I started working like crazy, idiot that I am.

"On Monday, the day before Christmas, he didn't come to work. We weren't really upset. It was amazingly warm, and we were able to make good use of the day, but we'd already long since filled all our quotas for the year. Besides, it was the first time Edgar'd been absent since we'd gone to get him."

That was just my luck, if you want to call it that. Just about the only thing that'd gone right. I still don't understand, for example, why I was so sure about my sprayer. But I was, in fact, more sure than ever. The idea with the hydraulics was about as logical as you can get. This vapor you got when you were spraying came from the air pressure. If it disappeared and you got the necessary pressure without air, then the thing worked. It was just too bad that I didn't have enough time to get myself the necessary nozzles. I had to wait until after quitting time, preferably till after dark, and then swipe Addi's. Addi's sprayer was lying abandoned under the trailer. My next problem was getting the necessary HP for the two pressure cylinders. Luckily I'd actually been able to scare up an electric motor with 2 HP. I even had to throttle it. I don't know if you can imagine what all two HP can cause when you let 'em loose. Maybe you think the whole thing was just a game or something. A hobby. That's BS. What Zaremba had said, that was true. That thing would've been a genuine sensation, technically and economically. About on the same level as front-wheel drive on cars was, if you know what that is. Actually a step up. It could have made you famous, at least in the profession. I wanted to slam it down in front of Addi and say: Just press on this button here.

I'd estimated that he'd just about flip. Then I could've straightened things out with Charlie and taken off for Mittenberg. I mean, I wouldn't *really* have ever slammed it down in front of Addi. It was slowly getting to be too big for that. It was slowly beginning to look like a wind-driven piss pump. I had everything I needed, only nothing fit together right. I just *had* to start botching it. Otherwise I never in my life would've finished. What I needed most was an electric drill. Besides that the motor naturally had three hundred eighty volts. I'd have guessed it was out of an old lathe. That meant I had to do something to jack-up the two hundred twenty in the garden house. I only hoped that the transformer I had was OK. I didn't have any kind of measuring device. That was probably another nail in my coffin. And the time to find one, I obviously didn't have that. And you just don't find meters lying around like old truck shock absorbers. By the way, you couldn't find them just lying around either, but you could at least get a hold of some if you needed 'em. Without the shock absorbers I'd have been all washed up. The casing actually should've been thicker, for the pressure. If necessary I was planning to bore out the nozzles. That would've made the stream thicker, but I wanted to start with oil-base anyway. By twelve I was so far that I needed the nozzle for adjusting. I took off in the direction of the construction site. I wasn't of the opinion that I was already done and that it would work on the first try. But this way I at least had the whole night for improvements. I was calm again. Mother Wibeau could've shown up at the earliest the next morning. She'd given me another chance. At the site everything was dark. I dove under the trailer and started undoing the hasp nut. Stupidly enough the only tool I'd brought along was the half dilapidated pipe wrench. Besides that, the nut was frozen. I almost tore half my ass off getting it loose. Just then I heard Zaremba in the trailer with a woman. I've already told you. I'd probably roused them. In any case, when I crawled out from underneath the trailer he was standing in front of me. He snarled: No?

He was standing right in front of me and staring at me.

Even though, he was standing in the light that was coming out of the trailer. He had this little axe of ours in his hand. Then I thought he was just blinded, by the light. But he had this grin in his pig slits. At *that* distance he must've been able to see me. Still and all, I didn't move a muscle. I can only advise you in a situation like that not to move a muscle. My opinion is that Zaremba was the last person to see me and that he knew exactly what was going on.

The whole way home I didn't see a soul. At this time of the night you might as well have been in Mittenberg. Generally speaking Berlin looked exactly like Mittenberg after dark. Everybody sitting in front of the boob tube. And the few hoods beating themselves to a pulp in some park or sitting in movie theaters, or they were athletes and were in training. Not a soul on the street.

By about two I had the nozzle in the socket. I poured about half the oil paint in the cartridge. Then I gave the switch a final checkover. I took another look at the whole thing. I've already told you how it looked. By normal standards it wasn't technically acceptable. But I was interested in the principle. I'd estimate that was my last thought before I pressed the button. I, idiot that I am, had actually taken apart the doorbell button from the garden house. I could've used any normal switch. But I'd taken apart the doorbell button, just so I could say to Addi: Just press on this button here.

I was a complete idiot, people. The last thing I noticed was that it got bright and that I couldn't pull my hand away from the button. That was all I noticed. It must have been that the whole hydraulic press didn't even budge. That must have caused the voltage to get enormously high, and when you've got your hand on it then, you can't get it off again. That was it. Take care, people!

"When Edgar didn't show up on Tuesday we went looking for him, about noon.

The police were on the property. When we said who we were they told us what had happened. Also that there was no point in going to the hospital. We were stunned. Then they let us in the garden house. The first thing we noticed was that the walls were covered with paint, especially in the kitchen. It was still damp. It was the same paint we'd been using on the kitchen paneling. Everything smelled like paint and singed insulation material. The kitchen table was upside down. All the glass was shattered. On the floor were a burned-out electric motor, hunks of bent-up pipe, a piece of garden hose. We told the police what we knew, but we didn't have an explanation either. Zaremba told them where Edgar had worked. And that was it.

We quit for the day. I sent them all home. Only Zaremba stayed. He started pulling our old sprayer out from underneath the trailer. He inspected it, and then he showed me that the nozzle was missing. We went right back to Edgar's garden house. We found the nozzle in the kitchen in an old piece of glass pipe. I gathered together what was still lying around, even the small stuff. The stuff that was screwed to the table too. At home I cleaned off all the paint. Over Christmas I tried to reconstruct the whole arrangement. A kind of jigsaw puzzle. I couldn't do it. Probably half the parts were still missing, above all a pressure tank or something like that. I wanted to go back to the garden house, but it had been leveled."

It was probably better that way. I wouldn't have lived through this failure anyway. In any case, I'd almost gotten to the point where I could understand Old Werther when he said he couldn't continue. I mean, I'd have never turned in my cards voluntarily. Never hung myself from the next tree or anything. No way. But I never would've *really* gone back to Mittenberg. I don't know if you understand me. That was

maybe my biggest mistake. My whole life I'd been a bad loser. I just couldn't swallow anything. Idiot that I am, I always wanted to be the winner.

"Just the same. Edgar's apparatus won't leave me alone. I can't get rid of the feeling that Edgar was on the track of something really sensational, something that you just don't think of every day. In any case, it wasn't just a tick. No doubt about that."

"And the pictures. Do you think that one of them could still be found somewhere?"

"The pictures. Nobody'd thought of that. They were covered with paint. They were probably leveled with the building."

"Could you describe some of them?"

"I don't understand that kind of thing. I'm only a simple painter. Zaremba thought they weren't bad. No wonder. What with his father."

"I'm not a painter. I was never a painter. I'm a statistician. I haven't seen Edgar since he was five. I don't know anything about him, not even now. Charlie, a garden house that's no longer standing, pictures that no longer exist, and this machine."

"I can't really tell you any more than that. But we can't just let his work go down the drain. I don't know what his mistake was. According to what the doctors said, it was something electrical."